VANTABLACK

ZETA

authorHOUSE®

AuthorHouse™
1663 Liberty Drive
Bloomington, IN 47403
www.authorhouse.com
Phone: 833-262-8899

© 2021 Zeta. All rights reserved.

No part of this book may be reproduced, stored in a retrieval system, or transmitted by any means without the written permission of the author.

Published by AuthorHouse 10/26/2021

ISBN: 978-1-6655-4287-6 (sc)
ISBN: 978-1-6655-4291-3 (e)

Library of Congress Control Number: 2021921963

Print information available on the last page.

Any people depicted in stock imagery provided by Getty Images are models, and such images are being used for illustrative purposes only. Certain stock imagery © Getty Images.

This book is printed on acid-free paper.

Because of the dynamic nature of the Internet, any web addresses or links contained in this book may have changed since publication and may no longer be valid. The views expressed in this work are solely those of the author and do not necessarily reflect the views of the publisher, and the publisher hereby disclaims any responsibility for them.

ONE

I wake up again before the lights of this bunker illuminate the streets I've been walking for years. I have two hours before the automatic lights turn on and everyone starts getting ready for a day in this metal cage. No one here seems to mind spending his or her life in this place—not that any of us have an option. The world outside was destroyed many years ago, before I was born. I can't remember the reason the war started. The elderly tell the tale, but they heard the story from their parents, who weren't around at the time it happened either. I guess after so many generations, everyone wraps his or her head around the idea that there's nowhere to go. I don't know what it is, but I can't shake the urge to just blow this wall down and go see the world that's out there, not caring how bad it may seem.

I walk the streets of this bunker until everyone else gets up. After so many years, it is normal to me. With so many people living here, I don't mind having the whole bunker to myself for a while. There's a certain freedom from having to push past people in the street or deal with the loud noise everyone makes.

I usually don't know why I wake up so early, but this time, I blame the anxiety I have been feeling for the last few days. I'm about to finally turn eighteen, or so

ZETA

my necklace tells me. They give one to everyone when he or she is born. With crime and fights happening all around, the authorities take hurting a minor seriously. We are basically untouchable.

From the day we are born, our necklaces start a countdown. Food and shelter are free until we come of age. Everyone else must either work for what he or she has or steal. Those who work go to the lower sections to farm or help with the animals.

This way of doing things, along with other circumstances I am not familiar with, caused gangs to form. To combat the gangs, eventually, a few people appointed themselves to keep the order and rules we all agree to follow. To announce their faction, the people protecting others wear the symbol of an elephant on their clothes, or they have it marked on their skin. They are the Elephants.

The gangs do the same; each group has its own symbolic animal. After countless wars among them, they agreed to designate areas that each group would control. They now reign supreme in their territories, and whatever they do is nobody's business, not even the Elephants'—if they stay in their areas, that is.

Long before I was born, there were so many gangs that they extended to each level of the bunker. After so many wars and fights, only a few remain. They all stay on the same level of the bunker. In the middle of all the territories, there is a big neutral zone that nobody controls, and that is the way it has been since I can remember.

After my necklace says I'm a man, I must get a job to be able to buy food and have a place to rest. I will work every day to stay alive and then sleep. Just

VANTABLACK

thinking about it makes me mad. I don't want to do the same as everyone else. I want more out of life. I want to live—to go out and feed my hunger for adventure. No job will ever give me that. So I've made up my mind: as soon as I turn of age, I will join the Wolves.

The Wolves are not as vile as the other groups. I already know a few of them from around the bunker, so it only makes sense for me to join. I don't want to be part of the other gangs, who let their members hurt people with impunity.

There are countless jobs to pick from here, but it doesn't make sense to me to live my life just to survive day by day. Why would I want to be alive in a place that kills my existence just so I can survive for a while? If survival is the game, I want to be able to do what I want without having to follow anyone else. I can't stop thinking about these walls, which they see as protection. It may be perspective, but I see a prison. I want to find my way. If I'm going to die eventually, I want to live my life. I try to see things from everyone else's point of view, but it doesn't make sense to me.

Marcus is a friend of the Wolves, but he has a panther as his symbol, which I have always found awkward. I don't know of a Panther gang around. Since I was eight, he has been a mentor to me. He lets me know how things are in here. I think it helps him remember too. He likes to fix the machines and components used by people who work in the lower areas of the bunker, both in farming and taking care of animals. When anyone has any technology to fix, he or she usually brings it to Marcus's establishment. He has always been good with electrical work and engineering and likes to show me. From time to time, he will create something, but he

3

ZETA

needs someone else to come up with the idea. He says that in order to have knowledge of a craft, you have to trade your creative side for each piece of information.

That's where his best friend comes in. His name is Gilligan, and they run the shop in the market section together. Marcus fixes the items, and Gilligan deals with the customers. Gilligan likes to come up with ideas no one has ever thought of. He gave Marcus the idea to reuse the necklaces—that way, the bunker doesn't waste more components and metal in manufacturing more. This has been a good business for them since resources around here are hard to come by. The people who work in the hospitals are grateful, and they receive low prices—not that they're happy about having to pay at all, but hey, nothing is free.

Marcus and Gilligan's shop is just a front for the Wolves. Every gang has its own. Even among the gangs, peace must be kept. Everyone must do something and earn his or her own. That's the only way everyone is content, and nobody starts anything to rattle the cage. With peace comes freedom for the gangs to take care of their real business under everyone's eyes. I'm still not sure what each gang has as a business, but they make enough not to have to work and to keep their members fed and happy. If that's not good enough for normal folk, too bad, 'cause that's good enough for me.

I'm an orphan here and always have been. After so many generations of violence and criminal activities, few have families. The kids from around here either are taken care of by their grandparents or learn the ropes of this jungle all by themselves.

Some of the people who make a living by taking care of kids don't have much knowledge on other aspects, so

VANTABLACK

they only teach the basics to kids: reading, writing, and basic math. We don't have anyone to teach everyone, so if people see something that interests them and that they wouldn't mind doing when their necklaces run out, they learn it. In my case, Marcus and Gilligan have the trade I've studied since I was younger. I'm not really planning on taking care of the shop and working like everyone else, but it's not a bad idea to be useful in something few people know about. My real plan is to get in with the Wolves and be part of their group.

As I walk the empty roads, I hear the loud sound of the lights turning on. So long to my alone time, I suppose. Time goes by fast around here. I guess that's why I always walk as if I'm in a hurry to go somewhere.

I arrive before everyone else to stand in front of the offices where they serve the food. I remember how soon I will have to pay for the food I'm about to eat. The workers from the food service usually get up an hour after I do. They have to get everything ready to serve so many people. Since I wake up before they do, I'm always the first. There's never a line for me. I simply grab my bag of food and go find a place to eat. This time, however, it feels different somehow. Sad. My last days of free food. I have always known how things are in here, but reality is just starting to sink in. I have three days of free food, counting today.

I've been trying to make some money for a month already. I only have enough for one day's worth of food after my time is up. I eat my sandwich as I walk and hide my apple in my pocket. I have to talk to Marcus and Gilligan and try to get them to help me be part of the Wolves. I figure if I start putting in the work now, I won't have to starve later.

ZETA

As I make my way to the market, the streets grow crowded. Everyone talks over one another. After all the noise comes the smell of many people gathered at once. After so long, one might assume I'm used to it, but I'm not.

The smell in the market doesn't get any better, with the meats for sale and all the people smoking. As I walk toward Marcus and Gilligan's shop, I smell metal and burned plastic. I see Gilligan smoking a cigarette while talking with his hands and moving around the shop as Marcus fixes a necklace.

Gilligan is a tall man in his late thirties, with long brown hair and black eyes. His face is always dirty, even when he never touches it. His beard is a mixture of brown and yellow. He always seems to be growing it out, but that's as far as it goes. I've always thought of him as energetic.

He turns to the street and makes eye contact with me. He signals with his hand for me to come to him. I speed up my pace.

Gilligan puts out his cigarette on some components on the table and then turns back to me with a smile and open arms. "So a few more days, and you are out of heaven. Have you given any thought to what you are going to do?" he asks.

Marcus, behind him, finishes with the necklace and throws it onto a pile. He takes his welding glasses off and turns around from his stool. "Oh, leave him alone. I doubt he wants to think about any of that crap yet," he tells Gilligan as he extends a hand. Gilligan rolls his eyes and hands him a cigarette and a lighter.

Marcus is about as tall as Gilligan. He has black hair that he always pulls back. Somehow, it always seems

6

VANTABLACK

wet. His eyes are as dark as the night. His facial hair always looks as if it's about to start growing—he says he likes to keep it short. He has a more serious tone than Gilligan. I've always thought of them as yin and yang: Gilligan is always energetic and carefree, and Marcus is forever serious and thoughtful of every step.

"I was hoping to talk to you guys about that. There's something I would like your help with," I say as I make eye contact with one and then the other. I take a moment to order my thoughts before asking as Marcus lights his cigarette. "I was wondering if you guys could put in a word for me to join the Wolves."

Marcus takes a long drag of the cigarette and exhales, taking his time with the smoke. He turns to look at Gilligan, who just shrugs and takes the cigarette from him. He takes his time in answering, which is good for me, since it means he hasn't rejected my request yet.

Marcus, with his hands on his hips, looks at the floor. After a few seconds, he lets out a sigh and picks up his head. He gives me a nod.

"All right, kid, we will let them know you are interested in a career with them," Gilligan says as he passes the cigarette back to Marcus.

I can't contain my smile. I feel sure I can make it into the group.

I decide to go walk around the bunker for the rest of the day to see what is happening. I make my way to my usual spot above the market, where I can see everything from above. I can watch all the people coming and going, and no one can see me—not because I am hidden but because people usually don't look up unless they are trying to find something.

One of the kids I know from around the bunker

ZETA

comes up to me. We don't spend much time together, since everyone is trying to figure out what to do, but we have become a little closer to each other recently since he is about to turn eighteen too, a day before I do. We are in the same boat.

"I got a job at the slaughterhouse as soon as I turn of age," he tells me, trying to make his way toward me without falling all the way down. I can tell he is scared of heights.

"Why did you pick the slaughterhouse?" I ask.

He shrugs in answer. I guess it is just something for him to do.

A lot of people do the same: they just pick a job, not caring what it is. It gives them a routine and helps them to get through the days. If they are fed and have a place to stay, that's all that matters. I can't picture myself doing the same thing. I want more out of life than just surviving every day and existing. I want a purpose. I assume that's what is driving me to try to make it with the Wolves.

I notice he can't get any nearer to me. He is shaking and trying to crawl. I decide to get off my perch. He follows me down, and we make our way into the streets. I take my apple out as I walk. I eat half and give him the other half.

"I found a crack in a wall. It's big enough for a person to walk through. Want to see it?" he says as he devours the rest of the apple.

I nod and follow him. It might seem as if a crack is nothing, but down here, that's the only entertainment we get. There isn't much to do. Everyone who isn't legal yet just explores or watches others work and do things.

8

VANTABLACK

There are not a lot of options for entertainment around here.

As I follow him, I notice Vultures in the alleys, going through things. Vultures are the thieves and criminals not affiliated with any gang. There are also old people who can't take care of themselves and hungry folks, but people tend to forget that. They are small groups, generally of four or five people, who commit crimes to survive. They don't carry any symbol. They just do what they have to in order to make it through the day. They are friends to one another and enemies to anyone who has something they need. They usually steal food or things to sell. They don't have a lot of people to rely on, since they usually burn a lot of bridges. They take care of one another and remain in small groups, their own miniscule chosen families.

I used to think they were people who went insane after not eating for so long that they let their instincts define their actions.

We pass the streets and alleys all the way to the outskirts of the bunker, where we meet the gigantic wall that imprisons us and keeps us from living but assists us in surviving. I don't like spending much time near the wall. It reminds me that there's nowhere to go and makes me feel as if my life doesn't matter. I don't like to feel that way, so I avoid being near the one thing that reminds me of those feelings.

I follow him. We finally make it to the area of the wall he wants to show me. There's a crack in the wall, just as he said. It's big enough for one person to crawl through it. Usually, someone reports such things to get them fixed or covered. Everyone is scared that one day, the bunker will give up, and we will be exposed to the

ZETA

poison of the outside world. We all have heard rumors of how things are outside.

Some say the air is toxic and melts your skin. Others think it paralyzes you and makes you stop breathing until you just lie there suffocating. Farmers say there's nothing outside, because nothing can grow, and if nothing grows, no one can eat. They say it's nothing but dirt as far as the eye can see.

We stare at the crack for a while. We can't see anything on the other side, just darkness. We talk about the different things we have heard over the years—about the world before the bunker and the world that is left. We exchange stories we have heard people tell. He tells me of an older man who told a few kids stories his family members have told each other through generations. The old man told about a time when women would go to the beach and wear revealing clothes, playing under the sun and doing nothing but enjoying a day with the people they cared about.

I have never seen the sun. It sounds like something made up. They say it's a big ball of radiating fire so far up in the sky that it shines on everything around it. I can picture only the lights of the bunker; they must be similar.

I tell him that according to Marcus, life outside the bunker wasn't really that different from life inside it. He told me there was more space, but everything was basically the same. Kids used to go to schools to learn things to later have jobs as adults. They played and ran through the cities.

I think Marcus told me all that to make me feel as if I'm not missing out on anything by being in here.

When we get bored, we decide to walk around

10

VANTABLACK

more. There isn't anything to do, so we exchange our theories about why we can't leave. After walking all the way to the other end of the bunker, we decide to head back toward the food service area. We are starting to get hungry again. I guess boredom makes your stomach work faster.

During the first food service of the day, I'm always the first, but the last two mealtimes always have lines of people, especially workers from the lower levels in a hurry to get their food and head back to eat. Every day there's someone in line who doesn't have a way to get food and either tries to steal from someone else or begs others to help him. No one ever does, since everyone is in the same situation. If they help him out today, they might be short tomorrow, and then no one will help them, so crying never helps.

I would like to say I feel bad for them, but I can't. I know that soon enough, I will have to fend for myself, and if I don't act now, when my time is done, I will be like them, begging to eat and having people turn their heads at me as I walk past while calling out in a voice filled with regret and desperation, knowing all hope for help is gone but still trying to find it.

I can't allow myself to worry about anyone else anymore. No one will worry about me.

I take my food when I make it to the front. I walk around the bunker as I eat my food. I have to find someone in need who can pay for any kind of service, so I can earn some money to get food for my future. Sometimes I find one or two people, and that's a good day. They won't give much, but it's a little more than I had before.

Today I can't seem to find a single person. I walk

ZETA

from store to store and living quarters. It's the same routine I've followed for the last month or so. I knock on the doors or approach others and give them half a smile as I look into their eyes. I look into their situations and try to find something they might not want to do that I can do for them.

"Would you like it if I cleaned your quarters? Do you need help with the children? Do you have any errands? Do you need an extra person to help out with work?" Like a broken record, I ask one and then move on to the next.

No luck today. Even if they don't want to do something, they would rather do it than pay someone to. No one here has money to waste over laziness. They will agree only when they are gaining more than they are paying for.

Sometimes I consider running errands for the gangs. They don't pay much either, but most of the time, they have tasks to perform, such as delivering notes and packages or picking up money that is owed to them.

The only reason I haven't done anything for them lately, even though I'm running out of time, is because I don't want the Wolves to question my loyalty. What would they think if they received a good word from Marcus and Gilligan to let me in and then found out I was doing side jobs for every other gang in the bunker? Loyalty and respect are important around here, second to money. If you run out of people to trust, you might as well become a worker, if they will still hire you. After that, all you can be is a Vulture.

All the workers from the lower levels are now coming back up to their quarters. This means there isn't much time left until it's lights-out again, when the day is over.

VANTABLACK

The market starts to die down a little. Most people go back to their families or finish up with their day.

Just like that, hours of the day have passed, and it's time to form the line again to pick up dinner. For dinner service, there are mostly old men and children in the line alone. This means they don't have anyone to cook for them or couldn't go to the market to get what they need to cook for themselves. So they come for dinner service. I see some of the kids turning eighteen today with tears running down their faces. The sight makes the ones getting close to their date want to do the same.

I can't cry. Not that I'm not sad or worried. I'm just too busy thinking of what I'm going to do tomorrow so I can eat when my necklace is done. A lot of the people here don't think of anything past a day or two, and the future catches up to them faster than they think it will. Their stomachs grumble. No one thinks about a plan to get food until he or she is already hungry, I suppose.

I finish my last meal of the day. I head back to my bed as the lights above me dim, and the streets clear out. My heart starts racing, as it does every night. It seems I will be sleeping late again tonight. Usually, my thoughts keep me awake at night. I can only assume it happens the same to everyone here. We are always worrying about what's going to happen.

I only hope the leader of the Wolves lets me into their group. If not, I will have to come up with something else to do. I guess that's what I'll be thinking of tonight: a plan B.

Two

I think I got only four or five hours of sleep last night. I'm not sure. I get out of bed and get dressed. The lights are still off, as usual. I have nothing to do, as I have to wait for everyone else to get up so I can start my day. I walk the streets with no destination, looking down at the ground the whole time. I'm not worried about getting lost. If I do, I can just walk in a straight line, and eventually, I'll hit a point I recognize.

All I can think about is whether or not I will be able to make it into the Wolves. My plan B is basically to ask Marcus and Gilligan if I can work for them at the shop. If I'm going to have to work either way, I might as well do it in a place where I know the people around me. I've thought about asking other gangs to let me join, but in a gang fight, I would hate to have to fight against Marcus and Gilligan. After all, I've known them my whole life. I'm closer to them than anybody else in this place. I've also considered applying for one of the jobs like everyone else, but those usually take a couple of days to get back to you or find you a place, and that means no food until my first pay. I know I would hate every second of it, but at least I wouldn't be hungry, I guess.

I look up from the ground for the first time since I started walking. I've made it all the way to the wall, and I'm right in front of the crack I saw yesterday. It's still here. I walk up to it without thinking anything of it. I look to find out if there's anything on the other side. I see only darkness. I stick my arm into the crack but don't reach anything. I decide to run back and steal a flashlight from one of the kids I know from the living quarters.

I run there and back. I don't know what has taken over me, but I want to know if there's something on the other side.

ZETA

I turn the light on and try to catch my breath before doing anything. I place a foot in the opening and lean in to see better. I shine the light, but I see only a long wall of concrete with darkness on the other end. It seems to go on for a while. I stop to think for a second. The only idea I have is to go inside and try to find out where the passage leads. If it leads nowhere, I can always crawl backward to get back.

I put the flashlight in my mouth and grab on to the wall to crawl inside. I start to feel scared and immediately want to back out, but I don't. I start moving forward. My head tells me to go back. I start thinking of scenarios in which this adventure goes badly for me.

What if I get stuck and no one finds me? What if the wall collapses? What if I die here? What if I die?

I ignore the thoughts by focusing on crawling deeper into the mystery this darkness keeps. It might be hiding something worth the trouble, or it might lead nowhere. Either way, I want to find out. My pants have started to get holes in them, and my body is tired. I think I should go back, but what if I'm close to the other end?

I keep going.

The flashlight's battery is low, and the light starts to flicker. I feel even more scared than before. I speed up, trying to beat the light. I have to reach the other side before it dies on me. It keeps flickering. I'm going as fast as my body allows me to. The light falls from my mouth, and I have to stop to search for it under me. The light has gone out. I back up a little and find it next to my feet. I can't bend to grab it, so I go back a little more. I hit the light against my hand to turn it back on, but the light is dim, with almost no power. I hold it in my hand and rush to crawl forward.

VANTABLACK

I keep going. The light dies in my hand. The fear I feel helps me go even faster. I feel as if I've made the biggest mistake of my life. I want to scream at the top of my lungs. My desperation pushes me to ignore the ache my body is feeling at this point. The fear is carrying me forward now, and I'm going fast. I close my eyes and keep rushing.

Finally, I arrive on the other side. With my legs still in the hole, I open my eyes, and my upper half is hanging close to the ground. There's a small light next to some stairs. I crawl over and climb out of the hole in the wall. I sit next to the wall, holding my chest, trying to stop hyperventilating. It takes me a while to calm myself down.

I get up and look up the stairs; they only go up. They seem to go as high as the lights in the bunker, maybe a little higher. I sit at the bottom of the stairs and rest for a second before I decide to go up. My right knee is scraped. It doesn't hurt, but it stings when I touch it.

I want to rest for a little longer, but something inside is driving me on. I get back up, look up, and pull my shoulders back before taking a deep breath. I hold it in for a second and then exhale slowly until all the air is gone. I take my first step toward what my gut tells me is the start of something important in my life.

I walk up flight upon flight of stairs one after another. My legs burn and shake. My body screams for me to stop, but I can't do it. The more I think about stopping, the more I feel as if this is a trial, and if I stop now, I will be trapped again and left to rot. I don't like that feeling, so I keep going. I keep going without stopping. I climb so many flights that my legs give up, so I crawl on my hands and knees.

ZETA

I finally reach the top of the stairs. My hands are shaking, and my whole body is covered in sweat. I make it to a door that is slightly ajar. I want to take a minute to rest before I go in, but I want so badly to see what's behind the door that I crawl over, place a hand on the door, and push. I fall face-first onto the floor as the door opens. I see a bright light. Then everything turns black.

I wake up with my head on the floor. It's hard for me to stand, and my arms and legs barely help me. The bright light is gone. I look around the room. I can barely see. I find a switch next to the door and flip it up. Light covers everything around me; it hurts my eyes for a second.

There are computers and electronics against every wall of the hexagonal room, except for two. There are buttons and switches all over the place. I don't touch any of them, since I don't know what they do. On the two walls without computers is a mirror that runs from one end to the other and is half the size of the wall. There is a desk in front of it, with more electronics.

I see cabinets, lockers, and several desks around the middle of the room. There are books stacked with papers and images. They look like drawings. I open some of the lockers. They all seem to hold different things. One of the lockers has bags inside that are cold. Another one has a few outfits prearranged on hangers. There are a couple more to open, but I go to the tables. I want to see everything, but I keep getting distracted by every new thing I see.

There's a small magazine with "Kept fresh for the future" written on the front and some images that look like the bags in the first locker. I open the magazine and start reading through it. Apparently, there is food in the

VANTABLACK

bags, and the bags come with instructions. As soon as I see the images of the food in the magazine, my stomach starts to growl. I run and grab one of the bags and bring it with me to the desk with the magazine. I start reading about how to eat it.

"It says to crack the sealed bag in half and wait two minutes before opening the bag."

I do as the magazine explains. I wait two long minutes and then open it. I slide the food out of the bag so I don't burn my hands. A small plate of steak with broccoli and mashed potatoes comes out of it. I can't believe my eyes. I start eating with my hands, not caring about burning my fingers or tongue. I devour everything. After a couple of seconds, my body starts to feel a little better. I guess it needed to recharge.

I walk toward the mirror to look at the tables. There's glass on the desks, and the glass surfaces have images running through them. I see a red light in the mirror out of the corner of my eye. I look up to see what it is. My eyes open wide with disbelief. The necklace I'm wearing is red. I touch the screen, and it turns off.

"My time is up," I tell myself in a soft voice.

I must have passed out for two whole days on the floor. I pushed my body to its limit, and now two days are gone. My new reality starts now, I suppose. I decide not to think of what will happen when I go back and just to look around. If a life I don't want is waiting for me when I return, I might as well take my time.

I tap on the glass on the wall, hoping it is a computer, but nothing happens. I have no idea what anything does, so I start reading the books and magazines around me for clues. I can't just sit here and hope to figure it out. I keep reading the magazine featuring the food, and then

ZETA

I'll decide what to read next. I have never read so much in my life. It's boring stuff, but if I don't read and learn about it, then this room might as well be empty. I keep going, and when I get hungry, I crack open another bag and read while I eat. After three bags, I fall asleep at one of the desks.

Suddenly, a bright light fills the room. It's not like the one that emerged when I flipped the switch in the room. It wakes me up as it shines from behind me. I rub my eyes and turn around. The mirror is shining brightly. I walk toward it. As I get closer, it becomes slightly easier to see through. I see a bright, deserted land. The sun shines down on it from far in the sky. There are clouds—like in the stories the elderly tell around the bunker. The sky is blue, as they've said. My eyes get watery. A tear falls down my face. It's the most incredible thing I have ever seen. The elders have described it many times and told many stories passed down in their families through generations, and I always have tried to imagine the outside world they describe, but my imagination has never come close to what my eyes are seeing.

The desert extends as far as my eyes are able to see, and so does the sky. I decide to sit there for a while and enjoy the view. Never in my life did I imagine I would see what everyone talks about.

I spend another day in the room, enjoying the food, forcing myself to read through books and magazines, and checking the view every couple of hours. It is a great place, and I don't want to leave, but I know the food will run out eventually, and I will have to go back. With that thought in mind, I decide to spend the day here and go back to the bunker tomorrow. I have to start moving forward with my plans back in my caged reality.

VANTABLACK

I wake up again, sitting at the desk. The sun hasn't come out outside the window yet. I decide to eat something quickly and clean up after myself. It is time to go back. I turn everything off and walk down the stairs. Halfway down, I feel the soreness in my legs, and I must crawl through the wall.

I make it back to the bunker, and the lights are still off. There is no one around. I make my way back to the place where I used to sleep, to recover the money I've saved and stashed away. It is hidden under my bed, in a secret opening I made. I am not allowed in here anymore now that I'm eighteen, so I break in quietly and carefully and get in and out as fast as I can.

Soon after, I walk the streets again, waiting for the lights to come on. I make my way to the market when they start illuminating above me. Marcus and Gilligan are probably opening the shop, I think, and I walk there.

I see the line starting to form at the food service. I am glad I decided to eat before I left. I don't have much money for food, so I have to save it for when I really need it. I see a man begging for food. It's always the same scene day after day.

I make my way to their place, and sure enough, they are there, discussing opposite views on any point Gilligan pulls Marcus into talking about.

"Did you guys talk to the leader of the Wolves? Will he let me in?" I ask, interrupting their conversation.

Marcus nods to me, saying hi. He then makes his way to his work area in the back.

"He said yes, but you were supposed to meet him two days ago. We couldn't find you to let you know. If we talk to him now, it will probably take a couple more days," Gilligan says, stroking his beard.

ZETA

I place my necklace on the counter, and he looks down at it. "I don't have a couple more days. Maybe one at the most if I don't eat much," I say.

He shakes his head, looking down. He scratches his head. He is thinking. I don't interrupt him. I know he is trying to think of a way to help me out. I wait in silence and walk to the other side of the counter. I place the necklace next to the pile Marcus has beside him to work on. He gives me a smile and turns around to keep working.

Gilligan lets out a sigh. "Come back at lunchtime, and we will take it from there."

I go to the food service until it is time to meet. Since I'm already here, I use my money to buy some food.

I eat on my way back to their shop in the market. I meet with Gilligan, and he tells me to follow him at a distance and not to make it obvious. We walk for about fifteen minutes, making turn after turn and going through back streets not a lot of people walk through. It gets to the point where I realize if I lose sight of him, I won't know how to get back to where we started. I wonder where we are going. Maybe he is taking me to meet the Wolves. If so, I don't know what I am going to say to get in with them.

Is Gilligan's word enough to get in? I don't know if wishful thinking is good for me at this point.

We finally reach a building, and he knocks on the door. He signals for me to come closer to the door with him. I speed up to catch up to him as someone looks out the peephole in the door. The man recognizes Gilligan and lets us in. We walk past several rooms on our way to a set of stairs at the end of the hallway. None of the rooms have doors, so I can see inside them as I make

VANTABLACK

my way behind Gilligan. In one room, two guys spar as more people watch them. In another, a man is smelting metal and pouring it into a mold. In a room right next to the stairway, I see a woman mixing liquids, with another woman groping against her from behind as a man sitting on a couch, bleeding from an arm and his head, lights a cigarette.

I'm confused, but I don't suppose I can ask Gilligan what all this is about. He would probably laugh without answering the question. We make it to the fifth floor. I see a bar close to the door, along the wall. It looks as if they tore down some walls and joined several rooms to make it. There are tables and colored lights everywhere. The walls seem covered with glowing paint. There are people dancing and having a good time. We walk past everyone to a corner of the room. I feel seduced by this lifestyle. For a second, I forget we live in a bunker. Maybe this is what they do to forget we are trapped in here: party and find someone to help them forget the existence we are forced to live. That and some alcohol might be enough to stay content in this place—not that there's a choice if one isn't content.

Gilligan approaches a table filled with people sitting all around. The man sitting in the center of the table gives Gilligan a nod. Gilligan nods back. Some ladies say hi to him. He smiles at them. I step up next to him to make myself visible. The man at the back has a wolf on his right shoulder. He is wearing a T-shirt with the right-side sleeve missing, as if to show his tattoo. He has a small scar on his left cheek, where the jawline starts. He has short hair and is clean shaven.

"How's your day going, Gil?" he asks Gilligan with a kind smile.

ZETA

"Oh, you know, it was going good until I saw your face." Gilligan laughs. "I'm here with an offering. He says he wants to be like you, Miles."

"Is that so?" Miles answers as he reaches for a cigarette.

"I would like to join the Wolves." I step forward, watching him light up the cigarette.

He inhales some smoke and blows it up to the ceiling. Then he looks back down at me. "Why?" he asks.

"I don't want to live like everyone else. I want my life to have meaning, and I want to do what I want when I want. Live by my choices and no one else's," I say with as much fire and passion as I can project into my words.

Miles takes a sip of the drink in front of him on the table. "Now, sounds to me like you are describing my spot at the table." He pauses. "Whether or not you are, there are rules even we have to follow. There's work to do around here, kid. You have to pull your own weight. It's like the system they have out there but with weapons in our hands while being chased if we step into the wrong place. We are like wild animals—a pack, if you like—and we take care of one another and protect our own from all the other predators out there. There's a lot of blood and pain necessary to protect what you care for. You sure you are ready to bleed for that?" He places the cigarette in his mouth again as he finishes.

I take a moment to answer. This life is different from what I was expecting, but I still don't want to go live a normal one.

"Guess I'll have to be better than everyone, so I don't bleed that much then," I say finally, hoping it sounds as cool as it sounds in my head.

VANTABLACK

Miles and Gilligan turn to each other and burst out laughing. I guess I must have sounded lame, or it wasn't believable coming from a kid like me.

"You know who he sounds just like?" Gilligan says.

"Marcus!" both say at the same time, pointing at each other.

I feel awkward at this point, so I wait for them to finish laughing instead of saying anything. They continue laughing for a while. Gilligan rubs his eyes after laughing so much he almost cried. They both let out sighs.

"I might have a place for you. There are a couple of small jobs coming up I might need energetic youth for. There might be a brawl in the process. You can show me then how good you are at the job. If you still want to be part of this life after that, you are more than welcome. Gilligan here brought you in, and I trust his eye. Let's see how well this plays out. What do you say?" Miles says with a crooked smile on his face.

I nod in agreement. Gilligan gets up and walks me back to the entrance of the building. He tells me he has to talk to Miles about a couple of things, and it is going to take a while, so I have to find my way back. Before I walk into the street, he gives me a marble, telling me that if it lights up, I should find him.

I walk all the way back to the market, to Gilligan and Marcus's shop, where Marcus is taking a nap. I don't want to bother him, so I just help myself. I grab a couple of things to make the marble into a necklace. Maybe it is because I've had to wear one for so long, but suddenly, it feels weird not to be wearing one.

I must be making noise, because Marcus wakes up. He grabs the necklace from my hands to look at it. He pulls it with his hands, and the chain breaks. He is

25

ZETA

closing one eye so the smoke from the cigarette in his mouth doesn't go inside it. He attaches another chain to the marble, pulls to check it, and then tosses it to me.

"That other crap wasn't as sturdy as this one. Now if someone pulls on it, he will take you with it," he says in a serious tone, but his words make me think it is a joke. I let out a laugh. He smiles back at me. I guess he can tell I have a foot in with the Wolves.

He allows me to help with the repairs of some gadgets and machinery for the rest of the day. He doesn't mind showing me how they work, and I don't mind learning. There isn't much for me to do until Miles calls me in to do a job for the Wolves. Marcus cooks some food for us, and we keep working for the whole day. The day goes by so fast that the next thing I know, it is time for lights-out. Marcus tells me he will close up shop by himself.

I make my way back through the crack in the wall and to the room all the way up the many stairs. I haven't had time to look for a place to stay yet, so I decide to use this room for now. I use some of the books as a pillow and lie on the floor, holding the marble in my hand, until I fall asleep.

Before the sun comes through the window, I get up. I continue to explore the room. I see some books that talk about the world and the different ways people used to live in it. It sounds incredible. All I can see through the window is a desert, but the book talks about beaches and oceans. Some places had ice instead of land. Others had many plants. The pages have pictures of the places and descriptions of the landscapes and how people lived. The book describes cities and countries. There were a lot of different things before life in bunkers.

I create a way to force myself into reading the books:

VANTABLACK

I will read one that explains things that can help me, using things from the room, and then, when I'm done with one of those books, I will read one I am actually interested in reading. It is taking me a while to figure out how this room works, but at least I am making progress, unlike before, when I would try to read one but would end up daydreaming and have to reread the same sentence over and over again. This new way, I trick myself with an incentive, which motivates me.

After a while, I can understand some of the computers in the room but only the basics. Some of the things in the room are there to help and create new things, which I find impressive, until I have to memorize how to actually do it. From what I can see, the room hasn't been used in ages. Maybe a couple of times when the bunker was being constructed and filled with people. Other than that, not a single thing seems to have been used. It's all new or almost new.

I see some clothes in one of the lockers, and I decide to try them out. I am able to wear only what is in my size—about ten sets of clothing, which is more than I could have hoped to have. The clothing seems to be gear for heavy tasks. A magazine describes it as *durable*. It is a military magazine, but the clothing doesn't seem like a military uniform. There are some watches among the clothing. As I read about them, I can't believe the innovations of the people who created them. Apparently, they can store up to one hundred items in them. All I have to do is grab a sticker and place it on an item, and it will break down the component and store it in the watch. It also comes with a huge warning that it doesn't work on living organisms.

There is also a backpack that does the same thing

ZETA

and has more space than the watch. I decide to use what is here to create a kit of necessary supplies in case I ever need one. I know it may seem a little paranoid, but I have always prepared for the worst, and so far, it has worked in my favor. I make one huge kit with everything I might need in case things go wrong and two smaller kits. I'm glad I have the resources to make them. In the end, I take everything from the room and store it in the backpack.

I keep going through the books and magazines, trying to remember as much as I can, learning all the knowledge this room will allow me to. The gear, the technology, and the computers along the walls—everything seems useful and mind-blowing. The only problem is that I can't show it to anyone. If I walked into the bunker and showed some of this stuff, people would want to steal it from me and sell it to someone or break it. I can't allow myself to enjoy any of it out in the open. Everyone would want some of it, and there isn't enough for everyone to have. It would create jealousy and discontent. I think of taking it to the Wolves so I can be in with them, but I know other groups would get word of that. It surely would put a target on their backs with rivals. So I do the only thing I can come up with: I keep it all for myself.

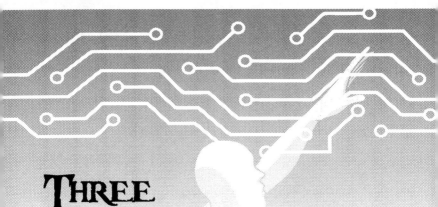

Three

A day passes, and there is no word from the Wolves. I have found a house to stay in while I wait to hear from them. There is only a bed, but that is enough. I don't plan on spending too much time in it. It is not hard to find a place to live in the bunker. There are many people, but there are even more rooms. Many are abandoned, and you need only to move in. If you don't have a key to the door, you can get a key from the people who keep track of the goods in the bunker. It isn't hard; they just send someone to check that no one is already living there before you move in. To make sure they don't get hurt or attacked, the offices will send someone from the Elephants as an escort.

After that process, I have my own place, and now all I have to do is wait for the marble Miles gave me to light up, so I can go see him. I can't help being annoyed by how slow things are going.

The day comes and goes, and nothing happens. At the end of the day, I go up to the room on the other side of the wall to watch the sun go down, and every morning, since I get up before everyone else, I go see the sunrise. I stay there for a while, read some books, and then go back to my room if I'm not too tired to go back.

ZETA

I do the same thing for four more days. I find myself on the last of the money I have to use to eat. I've already eaten all the food in the room, and now I do little jobs to get some money to eat. I should have rationed the food, but I didn't think it would take this long for them to call me in. Also, in my boredom, I got hungry a lot more, so I ate twice as much as I usually do.

It is morning, and I sit in my usual spot above the market, watching the merchants all set up their stores and shops, ready to start their day. I have my breakfast bag I picked up this morning from the food service. I decide to save my apple for lunch, in case I don't get called in and do not make enough to eat. I enjoy my sandwich as I watch those below me living their lives and going about their business as usual.

I can see Marcus and Gilligan's place from up here and notice smoke coming out of their shop. Some is from their cigarettes, which they smoke way too many of, and some is from the work they do to earn cash.

I have developed a routine over the past few days: wake up, see the sunrise, read a little, come back, eat, make some money if possible throughout the day, go back to see the sunset, read some books, and then go back to my room and start all over again. There isn't much I can do but wait for the Wolves to call me.

As I take a moment, as I do every day, to think of what I am going to do, I feel a small vibration. I look down, and the marble is shining with a low light. It is time to go meet Miles. I am excited and almost fall down while climbing back down to the streets.

Before I leave, I run toward Gilligan to ask him the way I should take to get there. I can't remember how we went the first time. He draws a map on my arm, and I

30

VANTABLACK

try to follow it as much as I can. It is not accurate, but it is better than my trying to remember all the turns.

After a while of walking all around the bunker, I make it to the building where they are. Miles is outside with a couple of other people. As I approach, they disperse. Miles says hi to me and grabs me by the shoulder as we start walking in the street, away from the building.

"You are going to start the same way everyone else does, kid. Nothing personal; it just won't seem fair if you are given special treatment."

I nod. I understand what he is trying to tell me. Just because Gilligan vouched for me doesn't mean I'll get a shortcut. I don't expect it to be easy or for them to give me everything I am looking for in life.

"You are going to shadow some of my guys here and there or just be an extra body in some jobs, depending on the situation. I just hope you are ready. It may seem a certain way from the outside, but once you are in, it's different. Reality hits a different way in this life. You might have to do some things you don't like. Some things you never thought you would. Sometimes the other groups or the Elephants might want to do some things to you that you don't feel you deserve. This is the life you are walking in."

He pauses to pull out a cigarette. "I wasn't joking about bleeding for what you care about. It doesn't matter who you are or how high you are in any of the groups, even the Elephants, who act like cops or military. We all have bled, and there's even more blood we might have to let run in these streets. If you are planning to live a long life without sweat, tears, and blood running from your head to your toes—and not just yours—this might not be the life for you. It's not for you if you want

31

ZETA

a peaceful life. We all go down sometime. It doesn't matter if you are a good guy or a bad guy; we all get pulled down to the ground. All you can do is hope you have enough to get back up, because the day when you don't have enough in you to get up is when the lights go out, and there's no coming back."

His tone remains serious, and I can feel some sadness in his words, as if he's thinking of all the things he's gone through to get to where he is. He is not just telling me this to scare me and have me back out. Every word has weight that he carries inside him and can't get rid of.

"You have to make up your mind and pick a lane. Take a moment, and come back to let me know what you want to do." He lets go of my shoulder and starts walking back to the building where we met up.

Before he can take another step, I give him my response. "Till it's lights-out," I say, looking at him.

He stops and turns back toward me with a smile on his face. He pulls the cigarette out of his mouth and puts it out by stepping on it in the street. He signals for me to follow him. I catch up to him, and he places a hand on my shoulder. He looks up to the ceiling of the bunker and then says as we make our way back, "Till it's lights-out."

We head back to his office. There, he sits behind his desk and gives me a paper with a list of places and names. He tells me to memorize them and collect money from them and tells me what they owe. He says not to leave without any money from them and not to let my guard down. "If it gets messy, get the money and run before the Elephants get there to interrogate everyone."

VANTABLACK

I remember his words "Information is important." I have to memorize the list and burn it afterward. If someone catches me, I should eat the paper and keep quiet, no matter what happens. I know this is not a game. I listen to everything he tells me, trying to remember as much as I can. I nod and only answer him if he asks me a question. Afterward, I make my way outside and take the first steps that lead me to my new life. There's no going back now.

I take a couple of minutes to memorize the top three names and addresses. After memorizing them, I tear up their names and eat the paper. I walk toward the first address, and I look for the person on the list. When he sees me, all I have to say is that it's time to pay up. He hands me a small bag. I do the collections three at a time. I get the packages and make my way back to the Wolves' building to drop them off. Then I run off to do three more. I have to complete the list the same day it is given to me. I have to run back and forth a lot. I could just collect all the packages at once, but if the Elephants see me, they will take me in on my first day. Worse, another group or the Vultures could find me and steal the money.

I don't know why all this money and these material possessions are being given to me to take back. I know only that I have to get them and deliver. I won't ask questions that don't concern me. I keep going like this every day, and each day, I get money in my pocket to eat for another day. It's easy money and quick too. I just walk around the bunker all day, collecting and delivering. I like walking. It is a pretty good workout. I also like getting paid and eating food. I really don't have

ZETA

to worry about anything at this point. It seems like a pretty easy way to live.

Unfortunately, all good things in life get interrupted by moments that don't go as they should, and they carry some extra weight in your memory once you recall them.

As usual, I walk around making my collections. I'm at the point where I can remember almost the whole list and get it done faster than before. As I deliver my last collections of the day, one of the guys from the building stops me on my way to the door. He walks me upstairs into the back room. I feel nervous. For the first time in a while, I feel worried again. I don't know what this is about, and I don't bother asking, as I know there would not be any response. I just go where he escorts me.

Finally, we make our way inside a dark room with only one light shining on a table, which Miles is leaning on. He has a drink in one hand and a smoke in the other. The room smells of cigarettes. He finishes his drink in one gulp and sets the glass down on the table. As he does so, I catch a glimpse of his knuckles. There is blood on them. With the hand holding the cigarette, he signals for me to come closer to him. I do as I'm told.

"There are moments in life that we would like to avoid." He exhales smoke with each word. "Moments we can avoid if we do the right thing or plan ahead. Then there are moments that other people force on us for no reason. Their own actions drive us there." He pauses to put out the cigarette in his empty glass. "This is one of the second kind. I would have liked to avoid this moment, but someone steered us into it. Without regard for what that would do to us or how heavily it would weigh on us. Still, that person will claim he is

34

VANTABLACK

the victim, even when he created this circumstance for everyone involved."

He walks away from me into the darkness as he speaks. With every word, my fear grows, and my anxiety crawls from my feet to my head like hands wanting to drag me down into the ground.

"This is going to be hard for you," he says as a light turns on above him, revealing a man sitting in a chair, bruised and bloodied. He isn't moving much. It seems he has given up hope and accepted his fate. Miles signals for me to come forward as he keeps talking. "You don't want this moment in your life, but this man has created the stage we are standing on now. See, things don't just happen to people. People make decisions, and each decision eventually reveals a moment. This man had no concern for this moment, as he didn't think it would happen. Now it's here, and he has dragged you onto the stage with him."

I stand close to the man in the chair, and I finally recognize him. He is one of the people from the list I collect from. I receive his payment and other things from him a couple of days a week.

"He has been short on everything he has given you. Not a lot. Just enough for anyone to notice, but if you add it all up day after day, it is quite a lot. Now, the reason you are here is because he handed the payments to you. At first, he said he paid in full, and he blamed you for skimming off the top from his dues. In time, he changed his answer, as he realized it wasn't going to make a difference to his situation. As you can see, his first thought was to drag you down so he could get out. He thought we are not that smart and that he was probably the first one ever to come up with that plan."

ZETA

I can't stand it anymore. My left leg is getting restless, and my right hand begins shaking enough for me to notice it.

"Since you are the one who collects from him, he becomes your responsibility, among the other ones and their payments, until someone else takes your place. Now it's time for you to decide what to do with him. I already did my part for what he owed me, and he understands that he still has to pay. The only thing left is for you to decide what's next. Do you give him a break, let him go home, and hope he never does it again? Which, if he does, let me remind you that would fall on you. Or ..." He doesn't finish that thought. He is going to leave it up to me to decide. "There's no place for 'Fool me once, shame on you' around here, kid."

I know what I have to do. I knew from the moment the light turned on and I saw him in the chair.

I would like to lie and say I don't do what happens next, but that's not the type of person I am. I don't lie about who I am and what I have done. I look at the man in front of me. A tear runs down his face over the dried blood on his cheek. In that moment, the person I have been my whole life disappears. The person I am going to become introduces himself to me. I can't feel bad for this turning point in my life. I have made the choices that led me here.

I walk out of the building as if nothing happened. The whole walk home, I can still hear the man crying and the sound of every punch landing. My body kept going by itself. The frustrations of my life, the fear, the anxiety, and everything wrong at the moment—I took it out on him. After I was done, I didn't feel anything. Nothing at all. I was just floating in a sea as I let go of everything.

VANTABLACK

Right and wrong don't matter anymore, because I have taken a path that is more wrong than right.

I go home and wash my hands before taking a shower. I don't go up to see the sunset today. I just lie here alone with my thoughts, trying to process what just had happened. I need my world to slow down for a second. I fall asleep after staring at the ceiling for a long time.

The next day, I go up to see the sunrise, as usual. I look up into the sky and imagine what it is like to feel the air outside this bunker, what the desert smells like, and how it would feel to be out there even for just one second, to stand in the middle of the desert I see outside the window of this tower. My mind keeps trying to imagine what it would be like to be out there, feeling the outside world. It is blank the whole time. Next thing I know, my mind takes me back to the previous day and what I did. I take a deep breath and let it out slowly.

As I look at the world outside, the words Miles said as he watched me leave the building appear in my head: "Find a way to deal with what you have done, because there's more to come. You might not have a chance to catch your breath in the future."

I make my way back after a moment and head back to the reality I leave behind every time I go up those stairs. My routine hasn't changed. Day after day, I do the same things. Things run smoothly, until they don't. What happened that day happens again from time to time. It is never easy to go through with it, but I do. All it takes is that first step, and my fists follow one after another. After a while, it is easier to move away from those moments after they happen. They don't completely disappear, but they don't hang in my head as often.

Four

I keep collecting for a few months, until one day, the Wolves move me into transporting and protecting cargo. I am glad, since I don't have to beat people anymore when they miss their payments. I only have to fight people trying to steal from us as we deliver whatever is in these boxes. I don't ask questions. If they feel I need to know, they will tell me. It is easier to deliver than collect, but there is more risk involved. We can't let the Elephants see us, or they will create problems for us. Some of them will turn away if there is some money going their way.

After finishing a delivery early one day and returning to the Wolves' building to get paid, I walk to the food service to get something to eat. I get some meat with bread and some vegetables. It is the first time I have eaten this meal from the food service. I have been saving most of what I make with the Wolves, and I don't really treat myself. Usually, I get the least expensive, most flavorless food. But for some reason, today I want something to make me feel good or at least make the day feel a little special.

I take my time in eating. I even sit at one of the tables in the food service area, which I have never done. I watch the line go, and one by one, people take their

VANTABLACK

food and go about their way. A feeling of being content comes back after months. It hasn't been present in a long time. I have been running automatically for a while, doing what they tell me to do without planning much ahead. I don't like that feeling.

Out of nowhere, I see a woman about my age step out of line with two bags of food. She has short dark hair, and her smile captivates the room, as if she has brought color back into the world around her. I leave half my food there on the table as I get up. I walk to a point where I can see her walk away into the street. She runs toward a couple of men sleeping on the other side of the street. She wakes them up gently and hands them the food. They thank her. One of them almost cries. I have never seen anything like it—helping others in a place like this. It is unbelievable. I want to go talk to her.

I walk outside the food service area into the street. By the time I am out, she has already disappeared into the public. I am left with just the memory of the moment when I saw her. A smile is on my face, though I do not notice.

I forget about my food and make my way to Marcus and Gilligan's shop. I haven't seen them in a few weeks with my new way of life. I tell them what I just saw, and they seem as impressed as I am.

"Must be that kid Zack's sister. I heard of her from a few other people a long time ago, but I didn't know she was still doing that," Gilligan says as he charges a customer in the front.

I sit on the desk as Marcus works. I pull a couple of apples out of my pocket, which I bought on the way here. I give one to each, and I eat the third.

"They say she is always working to make some

ZETA

extra money so she can help out whenever she can," Marcus says without stopping what he is doing.

"Odd," Gilligan adds, rolling his eyes.

"Odd? That's something unheard off. When was the last time anyone ever helped another person without wanting something in return?" I say.

"Well, she has been doing it for a long time now," Marcus says as he keeps working. "I think she has been doing it since she was twelve. She would make money by doing errands or helping with kids, and then she would spend it all on food to feed those who were starving. She didn't need the money since she wasn't eighteen yet. I think a couple of years back, she got mugged by some Vultures she was trying to help, and they tore her clothes and were about to have their way with her, but her brother found her before they did anything else." He is done fixing whatever he was fixing on the table and carries it to the area for completed projects.

I can't believe she is still helping people after going through something like that.

"Oh yeah. Isn't the brother part of the Fox crew on the other side of the bunker? I think he is their leader's right-hand guy. So nobody even thinks of pulling something like that now. He is very protective of his sister," Gilligan says.

I haven't made any deliveries that far from the Wolves' territory yet. The farther away a package needs to be delivered, the greater the risk. Sometimes crews will hand a package to another crew to hand to another crew until it reaches the person it is meant for. It costs extra, or sometimes it's a favor to be paid for later. The only reason anyone takes a package a long way is if it's very important and secret and if no one should see it other than the person it is for. Most of the

VANTABLACK

packages I deliver are things being sold or goods being exchanged—nothing important enough for anyone to lose an arm over but expensive enough that thieves might get beaten within an inch of their lives.

"Well, I just came to say hi. I'm going to go ahead and get lost." I say my goodbyes and make my way to the room on the other side of the wall.

I have almost finished reading most of the books and have found some things I can't wait to try out. Crawling through the hole and up the stairs isn't tiring anymore. I don't really break a sweat, as I did before. Sometimes, to make it more interesting, I try to sprint all the way up or take two steps or more at a time. I guess I have gotten used to the exertion by now.

I enter the room and walk in front of the lockers. I have seen the schematics of the room and know there are some things behind the lockers. I see a handle on the far left side. I push and then pull, as the manual instructs. The lockers move with ease. When they finally stop moving, I stand where they used to be. There are five metal boards hanging from the wall. As the manual explains, they are levitating boards that can be used as transport throughout any surface. However, they are only able to go up to twenty miles an hour and only four feet off the ground. I decide to modify them and then stick them in the backpack in which I keep everything else from the place. I have been cleaning out the room and also modifying some of the equipment I find. The modifications I make are always about the same thing. When the items were built, they included safety features so the user wouldn't get hurt. I find the safety features limiting, so I change them how I think they are supposed to be.

ZETA

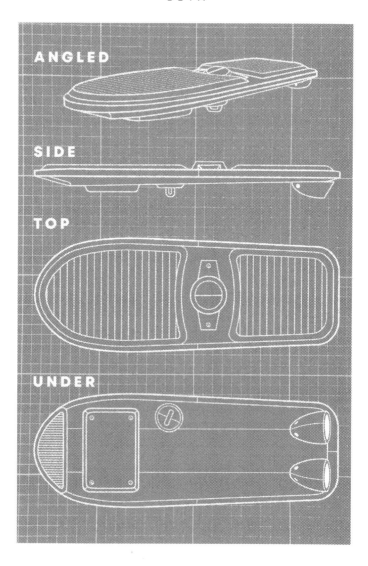

After modifying all the items, I pack them all, except for one. I need to make sure I know how to ride a levitating board, even if only in this small room. It is more about balance than anything. I fall the first few

VANTABLACK

times, yet after a while, I get the hang of it. It's one of the last items I take from the room and place in the backpack. I wait for the sun to set, and then I make my way back to my room. I hide the backpack under a heavy piece of furniture next to the door. I make a small hole to place it there so nobody will find it and steal it. I then lie in my bed and try to go to sleep. The last thing I remember before I close my eyes to sleep is the smile of the girl from the food area.

As usual, I keep making my deliveries or pickups, depending on the situation. I have a lot more free time than I did before. There are only four other gangs to deliver things to. Some of the other gangs don't ask for our services as of right now. The Elephants are more of a policing group. As of now, I only deliver to the Apes' and the Snakes' territories. They are the closest to the Wolves' area, and we have not had to make any important deliveries, or at least they haven't called me for those.

Every group or pack have their own things they sell or trade. It is all about who wants what and how much. Trades and exchanges go around almost every day—different goods from different places. Sometimes people get their hands on a little extra of something unaccounted for, and they make a deal to keep it going with a pack. They get extra money or something else they need as long as things stay the same. At this point, I still don't know what each pack has its hands on, but it must be more than one thing to have continuous trade going on. Packs trade mostly with their neighboring territories. That explains why I go to the Apes and Snakes so much.

Sometimes during deliveries, we encounter hired

43

Z E T A

Vultures. It would be bad for one pack to steal from another and start a problem between them, so what to do when you want something someone else has, but you don't want to take the fall for it? You hire someone else to do it. No names and no information, just the place at which to steal the things and where to drop them off. Everything about it is simple.

With so much free time on my hands since my promotion to securing packages and deliveries, I start to go insane—even more than usual. This place begins to crawl inside my head again, making me crazy about the fact that I have nowhere else to go. I don't know if it's because I have started to adjust to this way of life or because something inside me keeps screaming to be set free. I have to keep myself busy, or I'll end up losing it.

I go to the market whenever I've finished my work for the Wolves. I spend my time with Marcus and Gilligan. Marcus teaches me new ways to work with technology to fit it to my needs, and Gilligan talks nonstop. It makes the day go by faster until it's time to go see the sunset. The days keep passing by, as do the weeks and a couple of months. Nothing seems to change. I just keep myself busy as much as I can, trying not to get lost in the thought that I'm still in this cage. I go work with the Wolves and then go work at the market to learn more. I get familiar with the technology I found in the bunker and fit it to my liking, but I can't seem to find a way to fix myself to be happy. As long as I'm caged here, it doesn't matter what I do.

What a horrible joke life has set up for me. It has set me up in a cage and shown me the way to a window that shows me a world I cannot be part of. Day after day, I watch the sun go up and down. The wind moves

VANTABLACK

the dirt from the desert, and the clouds cover the sky with a different form day after day. The stars illuminate the sky next to the moon to keep some light in the dark until the sun comes back. I sit on top of the desk next to the window, dreaming about what it would be like to be on the other side of the glass. I know there's no use for it, but as long as I have that view, I forget I'm trapped inside. I forget that one day, everything I have done won't matter, and everyone will forget I was ever here. What a way to live.

I sit on the desk as I think about all of this. Suddenly, I see that I have been sitting on a screen the whole time. The desk is a computer. Somehow, it turned on. I climb down from it. It starts to make some noises, as if it wants to start working. After a few seconds, it lights up, and it stays still. I try to work it, but I don't know how to. There isn't a book or manual about a computer desk in any of the reading material in the room. I place my hands on top of it, and it seems to work similarly to the machines and computers Marcus repairs in the shop from time to time. I have to use my hands to drag the screen. It seems to show me a desert. I don't know what to make of it. I proceed with caution. I don't want to break it or mess with the program and make it unresponsive.

I move my hands about on the screen, changing positions and tapping on different areas. "It's a map," I say under my breath. The computer seems to be showing me the outside view of the world. It seems to be moving. I find a way to zoom in but not much. The screen seems to show me the outside world in real time. It only seems to go up to a certain distance on the view. I see a top view of the bunker and the tower in

45

ZETA

which I stand. They are surrounded by sand and dirt. The bunker is in the middle, and the feed of the outside world only goes up to a certain distance. I look around to see what is out there, but I see only dirt and a couple of mountains. I search every direction and find nothing worth watching.

Something catches my eye. I zoom in as much as I can, which isn't much. West of the bunker, almost all the way to the edge, there's a minuscule area with some green on it. I don't know what it is, and the image doesn't help me determine anything. I think it is vegetation, like flowers and grass growing—like the types of things one would see in the lower levels of the bunker.

We may not have a lot of things here, but we have to farm and feed the animals. I used to sneak into the lower levels, climbing from the metal beams above, to steal things from time to time.

That is what the image on the computer looks like: plants or flowers growing in that area. I might be wrong, but to my eyes, this is what it seems like.

I have played with the computer for so long I didn't notice the sun go down and the stars appear. I am excited, but I figure this can wait. The computer is not going anywhere, after all, and neither am I. I have all the time in the world.

Five

I make my way back to my bed, and I lie down to rest. I twist and turn in bed until I fall asleep. Tomorrow will be another monotonous day. Like always.

"This is an important package, so I need it to arrive safe and in time," Miles says as he places a four-foot-tall package in a tall, slim bag so I can carry it as a backpack. He places the package in my hands without breaking eye contact. "If this goes as planned, we will have more packages to deliver than before and a lot more money. Be careful. Don't stop for anything. As soon as you walk out that door, you go as fast as you can without getting any attention. I'm trusting you with this."

I can tell he is letting me closer now than ever before. Slowly, I make my way inside the inner circle of the Wolves.

I close the door behind me as I leave the building. I make my way toward the neutral area in the center of the bunker. I am on high alert the whole time, and I haven't even left the Wolf territory. I can't fail. I haven't done so yet, but there is no way I am going to with something this important. I am almost to the neutral area.

I am just a couple of streets from the neutral zone, when a couple of Vultures wearing hoodies approach

ZETA

me from behind. One pulls me by the shoulder and, without hesitation, punches me in the face. Their faces are covered. There are two of them. The other one reaches to grab me, but I am able to stay away. Adrenaline races through my body. My left leg grows restless, and so does my left hand. I have encountered fights before while delivering other packages, but this time, I am all by myself. No sense in asking for a fair fight.

The Vulture on my right tries to circle around me, trying to stay away from my view. I turn toward his friend, making it easier for him. I have a feeling he is going to try to grab me from behind. He does. The moment I feel him grab my arms from behind, I throw all my weight behind, forcing him to step back with me. I slam him against the wall behind us. I can tell he receives a big hit in the head because of it. His grip loosens, and I am able to escape his grasp. The other one stays in front of me, watching everything happen. His eyes widen.

As he sees his friend sit on the floor while grabbing his head, he panics, pulling a knife from under his clothing. He is shaking. The sight reminds me of the first time I had to fight during a delivery. Is this their first time trying to rob someone? It doesn't matter. We are here, and their actions make it seem as if they are inexperienced with the situation. He quickly takes a step forward, attempting to stab me. I move to the side and hit him in the face at the same time. As he falls to the floor, his friend seems to have stopped hurting from the blow he received a second ago. I rush to grab his knife as it falls out of his hand when he hits the floor.

VANTABLACK

Both stare at me now as I hold the weapon. They don't know if they should stay or run.

The Vulture I grabbed the knife from runs. I can see the look of betrayal on his friend's face as he watches his partner run. He decides to stay, pulling his own knife from his clothes. He isn't going to give up. He gets closer to me slowly with his knife pointed at me. He takes small steps, cautious not to make a mistake. I don't move. I am waiting for him to attack me to react. I have to remain calm. I can't act erratically and let myself get stabbed.

He is tense. He moves his hand quickly in short motions with every step he takes, as if trying to keep me on my toes by changing the position of the weapon. I do not look at the knife. My attention is on him and his body. The knife isn't the problem. The knife is just an accessory, an item, a tool. He is what I need to stop. When he gets close enough to me and there is nowhere to go, he stops. He is shaking still. He takes a huge step forward, trying to stab me. I am able to move back and grab his hand. Without thinking about it, I lean forward, stepping close to him. My body is in front of him as I hold on to his hand with the knife.

He falls to the ground. I have stabbed him in the chest. He loses all will to fight. He just lies there on the ground as the blood escapes his body, coloring the street. I look down at my hand, and it is shaking but not as much as before. The knife in my hand is covered in blood. I can see a few drops of blood on my clothes. I place the knife next to his feet and turn all around me. No one has witnessed this.

I keep walking on my way. My heart is beating fast,

ZETA

but my body doesn't shake anymore. I pass street after street, heading toward the neutral zone.

The neutral zone is one of the most crowded areas in the bunker, second to the market. As I step into it, I can see even from where I stand that somebody has told everyone about this delivery. I can sense all the eyes that want what I am carrying. There are small groups hiding among the crowds, staring at me, watching the steps I take. None of the groups have an animal on their clothing, and their faces are covered. They are coming to get me. I can't go back. The only direction is forward, through all the obstacles in my way.

I take a deep breath and let the air flow slowly out. I take my first steps. I have to look out for all the groups at the same time. I have to come up with a plan too. They haven't made a move yet; they are just following me at a distance. They probably can tell I am aware of their presence. I see two guys from the Elephant militia patrolling the area. I get closer to them and follow closely. No one will make a move with them around—unless they are thinking about taking them out too. I still haven't come up with a plan yet. My thoughts are still scrambled. I keep my breathing in check.

I inhale deeply, pull my head back, and look up. There it is—my plan. From the excitement of coming up with it, I start coughing as all the air comes out of my lungs at once. The Elephants in front of me turn their heads as they keep walking. I give them a smile once I stop coughing. I try to hide the fear I am feeling at the thought of them noticing the bloodstains on my clothes. The stains are obvious to me but apparently not so much to them.

I notice that everyone following me stops when the

VANTABLACK

Elephants turn their eyes toward me. I wait to start my plan. I can't do anything while I hold their attention. Finally, they look at each other and then turn their heads forward again. As soon as I am out of their eyesight, I run.

I have to lose my pursuers fast. I can hear them behind me, running fast, pushing over people, creating chaos to reach me. I make my way to the upper floor of a building. I know exactly where to go. I am going to reach my destination by running above everyone, using the metal structures that hold the lights together. I just have to lose my stalkers first to make sure they don't follow me.

I am on the second floor of a building in the neutral zone. I run as fast as I can without hurting anyone. I have to make my way through. They are behind me, catching up. A couple of them are able to get in front of me and cut my path. I have to think fast. I jump from the second floor onto the cloth roof of a shop. The roof collapses with the weight of my body. I land on my back. I get up quickly and make my way to the other side of the street, through all the people in my way. I make it into another building and run all the way to the top. I can see them from up here, running into the building, trying to catch up. From the top of the building, I should be able to get onto the structures that hold the lights of this level of the bunker.

Once I'm up here, all they can do is look for me. Even if they see me, it will be hard for them to catch me. I can run through these structures without looking down. I have used them all my life to move through the bunker, since I have always disliked the overly crowded streets. I can't believe it took me so long to think of it.

ZETA

By the time they are able to reach the top of the building, they can't see me from that distance. Now I can use this route to reach my destination without encountering any more setbacks.

Somebody must have talked, because everyone seems to know that what I have is important. They followed me, so they knew the day of the delivery and knew I would use the neutral zone as a route. I have never seen so many people want a package I have to deliver. I have heard of it from other Wolves, but I never pay attention to them. I always imagine they exaggerate to make their stories more interesting. But some of them must have been telling the truth, since I am going through it now.

I manage to reach the Tigers' zone. This is where I have to deliver the package. I have to go into the streets again. There aren't many lights in any of the pack zones. Most of the structures that hold the lights have been removed. Most packs have taken them down and used the metal to make weapons, since guns are useless. Gunpowder is hard to come by. Most take the powder from bullets to sell or use for other things. So if someone ever is found with a bullet wound, everyone knows that the person who shot him really hated him. Some guns are melted to make swords or other weapons that don't have a limit on their usefulness.

I make my way down the building closest to the Tiger pack's building, down the stairs, and into the street. I keep my head down, trying not to attract any attention. I keep looking back to make sure no one is following me. I keep going at the same pace so as not to appear as if I am in a hurry. After a while in this job,

VANTABLACK

I realized the things that give someone away to people when he or she is trying to appear normal.

I finally make it to the building. There are two guys protecting the entrance. They stare at me without saying anything.

"I'm here to deliver a package," I say. I remove it from my back and place it in my hands, trying to give it to one of them. They just look at me without touching it. One of them opens the door to let me in. They must have been expecting me.

I walk inside. They have poor lighting. Most of their lights are red, and a few are white. It is as if their whole theme is the color red. All the doors are closed. I can only assume they are very secretive about what goes on.

I keep walking until I make it to a big open room. A man waits for me. He has his face covered. He looks at me and gives me a signal with his head to follow him. He walks me to the back of the building. I feel nervous but not as much as I was in the streets with this delivery on my back. He opens a door and steps to the side, holding it for me to walk through. I do as I am instructed.

Inside the room are two men. One is wearing a jacket with a tiger on the back. The other is a boy about my age with a tiger tattooed on his forearm. I hear someone flip a switch. The red light is gone, and light from a regular lightbulb takes its place. Everything is more distinguishable now. All around the room are unsealed crates and a few tables that seem to have been cleaned in a hurry.

The man with the tiger jacket signals for me to come closer toward them. We all approach the table simultaneously. I place the package on the table and

ZETA

take a step back. The man smiles. He unwraps it and pulls the contents out of the package, revealing a sword. I don't think much of it. Some people here prefer to carry swords or other weapons for protection. It doesn't matter if you are part of a pack or not. Swords just happen to be less easy to conceal. Sometimes the streets are too crowded, and fighting with a sword can be a problem.

He admires the sword for a second, carefully looking over every detail. Eventually, he presses something in it that makes it heat up. His companion pulls out another sword and takes a defensive stance with it. The man swings his sword and breaks the other one. It goes through swiftly like a heavy rock on water. The other sword could have never stopped it. The man can't stop smiling.

"Tell Miles that Julius is happy with the product," the man with the tiger jacket says as he keeps admiring the sword.

I assume his name is Julius. I am not wrong. The sword starts dripping. A small drop falls onto the table, piercing it just after landing. It's acid. Swords like this are similar to the weapons I found in the secret room. However, these weapons are more primitive. They have power, but they can't contain it properly, so the materials they use will leak out slowly, making the weapons work until they run out of juice. After that, they become ordinary like all the other ones and maybe even more fragile. Julius doesn't seem to care. Apparently, they are the best thing to go with right now.

VANTABLACK

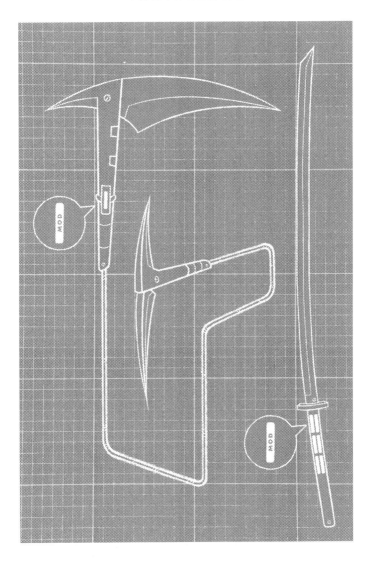

He puts the sword back in its place after powering it down. I don't like the look in his eyes. His eyes seem full of insanity. Julius has a strong, slim frame. His long brownish-blond hair is pulled to the back. He is clean

ZETA

shaven. There is something about him that makes me uneasy. I don't trust anything about him. His smile seems villainous. He doesn't seem to speak unless he has something to say. It makes me feel as if he is planning something even as we stand here in silence.

He thanks me, and I go on my way after that. I make my way back toward Wolf territory with more ease now that there is no reason for anyone to take me on. It's weird, but even as I walk away and find myself in the neutral zone, I still feel Julius's malevolent aura near me. There is something troubling about that man. I just hope I never have to find out what.

I make my way toward Marcus and Gilligan's shop. There I see one of the guys from our pack. I tell him to pass the message to Miles that the package has been delivered. He nods at me and goes on his way. Marcus offers me a drink, and I take a seat inside the shop.

I drink from the lemonade he hands me. I wait until Gilligan is done with one of the customers to talk to them about what just happened. I ask them about the man named Julius, whom I just met. I explain to them the weird energy he gave me the whole time I was around him and even on my way back. They know exactly who I am talking about.

"He is one malevolent guy—I'll tell you that. Most of the members of his pack are scared of him. To anyone else, he seems charismatic and normal, but for people like us, who have been on this for a while, we can sense the evil inside him leaking out. He might try to contain it, but he isn't able to. I don't know what it is. It's like we have an animal sense that makes us able to feel it. That's as best as I can describe it." As Gilligan talks, he uses a lot of hand gestures, as usual.

VANTABLACK

Marcus just nods the whole time. I listen. Oddly, I understand what Gilligan is trying to say. It makes sense in a weird way.

Marcus takes a sip of his lemonade and then sparks a cigarette. I know he is about to say something. He likes talking with a cigarette in his hand.

"Whatever you do, don't get comfortable around him, no matter what. If you let your guard down, he will take you down. He hasn't been in power that long. His father died a couple of years back. Word was that he liked to smack Julius around and was harder on him than anyone in their pack. They say it was because he needed to earn the crown of the pack. He didn't want the others to think it was given to him just because they were related. His old man was crazy."

"Didn't his father treat their pack like a cult whenever he killed the last guy running it?" Gilligan asks, interrupting.

Marcus nods in agreement. "His old man was crazy, and there is no exaggeration at all when we say it. He had some weird beliefs. The members of a pack get a tattoo or wear the symbol on their clothes, depending on personal choice, but that man would personally carve it into them one by one. No one was allowed to leave after they were in, no matter what."

"Julius's father had the idea that there were rich folk among us. That some people weren't pulling their weight in the bunker. He would yell that there were more people than we knew in here and claimed that was why no one ever had enough food. Other times, he would claim that someone was trying to steal his brain since he had all the answers. Story goes that he lost it in the end. Wouldn't trust anyone. Supposedly, he ended

ZETA

up trying to kill everyone in his pack. He injured a few folks, until Julius had to put him down. His own father. That's some hard shit. Doesn't matter how bad he might have been to him," Gilligan adds.

"Whatever you do, get in and get out. That man is evil and might be crazy like his father. I just hope we never have to find out. He seems smarter than his pops. A real thinker. Smart people always make the hardest villains. Be careful," Marcus says, getting back to work.

I finish my drink, leave the shop, and go up to the room outside the wall to see the sunset. As I watch the light of the sun go down, I think of what Marcus and Gilligan said. The memory of Julius gives me chills. No wonder the guy with him in the room didn't say a word or flinch when he tried his sword against his. Julius must have the pack scared, just as his father did. He must run a tight ship.

It's getting late, and I am tired. I decide to call it early today.

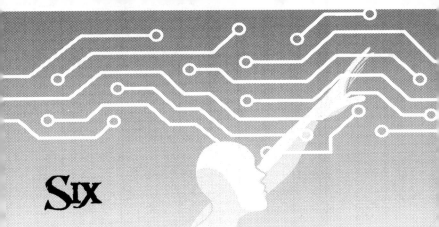

Six

I wake up a little late the next day. The marble Miles uses to call me in is on. I don't know how long it has been this way. I make my way to see him. I don't stop for food or anything. I don't even think about eating in the rush I find myself in. I run up the steps to meet him on the second floor of the building.

I apologize once I get there. He doesn't mind. If someone isn't here to do a job, someone else picks it up. The train keeps moving no matter what. Only if no one answered the call would he have a problem, but that would never happen. He has a girl who keeps track of everyone doing deliveries and to whom and where. If someone is available, she knows about it and calls him to go do what needs to be done. Once you are in, you do a little bit of everything occasionally. The Wolves only let in people they trust, so they don't mind being patient while everyone learns the ropes, in case someone has to take over for anyone else.

Miles gives me the rest of the day off. He has only some small jobs here and there and doesn't need me for them. He never makes me feel as if I am in trouble or as if he is reprimanding me. If Julius is crazy and malevolent, Miles is the opposite. He knows how to lead people without fear. He maintains neither a tight

ZETA

grip nor a loose one that would cause it all to fall. He knows when to give slack and when to keep it. The more I learn about him, the more I can tell he really cares about every Wolf in his pack. He isn't looking for followers or workers. We are his friends, and we respect each other. He treats us like equals and makes us feel like we matter. That is hard in a place like this. I always wonder why he hasn't had children, when he has all the qualities for it. Many other unqualified bastards in this place sure have a lot of their own.

As I walk out, the lady who helps Miles informs me that another guy is making the delivery they called me in for. Apparently, it is to the Fox territory, right in the middle of the Tiger and Snake packs. I haven't been to that territory yet to meet with the main guy, and I would have liked to go, especially since the girl I saw at the food service might be there.

I make my way to buy some food since I haven't had anything to eat yet. As I stand in line, about to get to the front, I see her again. She has three bags of food in her hands. One is for herself, and she is giving away the other two. It still surprises me, even though I saw her do it before. Maybe it's because I am so used to nobody helping anybody in here.

When I get to the front, I keep looking back. She is sharing her food with an old lady on the street selling handmade tools and clothes. Anybody can see she doesn't have much, as her selling isn't going well. I buy six sandwich bags with fruit. I walk at a fast pace, trying to get to the girl.

When I finally do, I become nervous. I don't know what to say. As I am about to cowardly talk myself into not talking to her, she turns her head. I feel my face turn

60

VANTABLACK

red, and my mind runs as fast as my heart. She smiles and, with a friendly voice, asks if she can help me with something. I raise my hands, showing her that I have a few extra bags of food for her to give away, plus one for myself and one for her. I can't get my mouth to produce any sounds. Luckily, she understands. She tells me to follow her, and without question, I do. I walk behind her the whole time as she leads me where she wants to go.

We walk around in the street for a few minutes. If she sees others begging or feels they haven't eaten, she introduces herself if they don't know her yet. Then she places the bags of food in their hands and gives them a smile. Some of the people in need she already knows from before. Others are complete strangers. It makes no difference to her.

After each bag she gives away, she turns toward me, tilts her head, and smiles. Her short hair covers little of her face. Her smile seems to shine as brightly as the sun in the room I spend many days in. I see that her eyes are different colors. One is green, with thin lines of brown or orange—it makes me think of the gardens on the levels below, around the working areas—and the other one is blue like the sky. I almost feel as if I am looking at the sky.

The whole time, I haven't said a word. By now, I can only assume she thinks I am a mute. Bag after bag she gives them away. I don't pay attention to anything around me. All I can think of is what I can say to her. I don't know where we are going. I just follow, focusing on her without being a creep.

My thoughts don't catch up to us until she tries to give a starving man a bag to eat. He doesn't want it, though it is clear he has not eaten in several days.

ZETA

His mouth starts watering when she tells him there is food in the bag. But something—maybe pride—stops him from grabbing the bag. She keeps insisting, and he keeps denying. She will not take no for an answer.

"I've told ya before, kid. Stop bringing me food. I don't want anybody's help. Okay?" This bone of a man obviously knows her from before.

"Well, like I have said before, as long as you are starving and I can get my hands on food to give, you will keep dealing with me," she says assertively. "If you want me to stop helping you, show me you don't need help, and I'll go away."

The man finally gives up. She hands the last bag to him. He pulls out the sandwich and starts eating it with attitude on his face. It seems funny to me, so I let out a laugh. She turns around and thanks me.

She gives me a smile and introduces herself. Shanti is her name. It sounds magical. I have to remember to look away from her so I don't make her uncomfortable. She can tell I am interested in her. I'm not good at hiding it, especially since it takes me a while to introduce myself after she does. I feel strange. I want to get to know her and hopefully see where things lead. The only problem is, I have no clue how to talk to her. I'm barely able to sound out my name.

We walk down the street side by side. She doesn't mind the silence. I think she is waiting for me to gather myself and find something to talk about. I need to breathe slowly and start talking, or she is going to go away. I ask her why she does this. I mention I've heard she has been doing it for years now. I am lucky she doesn't find me weird for knowing a few things about her, when she knows nothing about me.

VANTABLACK

"I know what it feels like to be hungry. I don't want others to feel that way. If I can help someone, I will," she answers.

It is a simple answer, but it says a lot. I don't ask her more on the topic. She asks me why I do it. I don't know what to say. I haven't had time to think about anything from the moment I walked up to her. I suddenly realize she has given away even the bags I got for her and for myself. It takes me a moment to answer her.

I answer honestly and tell her it is my first time ever doing something like this. I tell her I saw her giving away what she had and felt I should help her out. I also tell her that I am interested in her and that the sight of her blew me away the first time I saw her. I guess the nerves I am feeling have found their way to me, because I don't mean to say it, but I do. She smiles and tells me she appreciates my honesty. I am glad she hasn't run away already.

We spend the rest of the day walking and talking. She does most of the talking; I just ask questions and give my opinions here and there. Since she likes honesty, I don't lie to her when she asks me where I work. She understands how things run around here. After all, her brother is the right-hand man for the Fox pack.

We keep going until lunchtime. We sit in the food service area. I convince her to sit and eat with me at the table. I promise to help her buy some food and give it to people in need after we eat. It is the only way I am able to get her to stay longer. The conversation becomes more profound as we eat. She asks me about the area I grew up in and how I got to where I am. She seems to enjoy listening to what I have to say. I can tell since she

ZETA

has already finished eating but hasn't run off to go save the bunker. I start to feel she is also interested in me.

After I finish my food, I buy more, and we go back out into the street to help a couple of people who haven't eaten today. I ask random questions I can think of. I enjoy hearing her voice. Her way of viewing the world is realistic. I don't expect that from someone who seems so hopeful. I avoid the topics of the packs and her brother. We are enjoying the moment, so I don't want to talk about something that will burst the bubble we've created around us.

At dinner, she doesn't deliver anything. We just sit in one of my usual spots above everyone in the street, drinking lemonade. I tell her I want to leave this place. She feels the same way, but she can't imagine what leaving would be like. We share stories about what we have heard about the outside world and how it came to be. I guess it doesn't matter where one grows up in the bunker; everyone's stories are crazy. No one knows what happened. People have been in here for so long that everyone just shares made-up stories about made-up stories. The more we share, the more it makes us laugh. We laugh until it is so late that almost everyone has already made it home. We don't notice when the streets under us are almost empty.

I walk her all the way to the Fox zone. I walk a couple of streets past it before I notice where I find myself. I don't know what it is; I just know I'm willing to risk the trouble I might get in if I keep going. She seems to be worth the trouble. She smiles at me again before saying goodbye. She tells me she'll try to see me again tomorrow or whenever I can. She wants to spend

VANTABLACK

more time with me. That's when I know she feels the same way.

I smile the whole way back to my bed. I don't even remember the room atop the stairs. It feels crazy how everything around me disappears around Shanti. There are times when I forget the bunker caging me inside it. I keep thinking about her until I fall asleep with a smile on my face.

The next morning, I make my way to the room. Since I have time, I head over to satisfy my curiosity about the green area on the map. I need to know what it is about. I scroll through the map and find it. It is smaller than before, but it is there in the same place. I wonder what happened. I can only assume some of the plants died. The large area has been reduced. I don't think I would have been able to see it if more had been wiped out. I am intrigued by what is happening there. In the end, it doesn't matter. I can't do anything. The world out there is uninhabitable, and there is no way out of this cage that provides us shelter.

I decide to wait until the sun comes out. I can still see some stars disappearing as the rays of the sun come to cover them and take their place. I make my way back to the Wolf building. Something is making me feel uneasy. For some reason, sadness surrounds the room, even with the beautiful view. I don't know if it is because I am unable to leave or if seeing those plants try to make it just to be swept away has upset me. I go on my way.

As usual, I do my runs, anything Miles has for me. It distracts me from what I was thinking or feeling before. I make sure to stay busy for the rest of the day. On my way to a delivery, I see Shanti helping others. She is too busy to notice I am around. I walk up to her

65

ZETA

and say hello. It seems the sight of her erases all the bad thoughts and feelings in my head. Since I am still working, we agree to meet at the end of the day for dinner. She tells me she would prefer to make food. I tell her we can use my place. She agrees. I tell her where I am staying. She says she will pick up some things on the way to cook. We smile at each other and then go about our day. I keep on with my usual routine.

After my last delivery, I make my way to say goodbye to Miles. I am going to meet with Shanti and don't want to be late. I give him the bag from the delivery, and he smiles at me as he grabs it. I look to his right, where a woman is sitting. It's his girlfriend, Eleonore. I have seen her around but never talked to her. She takes care of kids and teaches them how to read and write, among other things. They have been together for a long time, before I arrived or turned of age, I think. Everyone can tell they love each other. Miles is friendly, and he can be hard, but with her next to him, he can only be happy. She smiles when Miles looks at her.

I ask them what is going on. I can tell Miles is making fun of me, but I don't know the reason.

"You haven't been able to stop smiling all day. When the day started, you were serious and blue. After a while, you came in smiling to drop a package and haven't been able to stop," Miles says.

I didn't notice my smiling.

"He is in love," Eleonore says.

I don't know what to say. Miles laughs. Eleonore walks toward me and gives me a hug. I can tell they are happy for me. I tell him I am ending my day. He knows I am going to go see her. They look at each other and smile some more. I have to get out of here quick.

VANTABLACK

I speed-walk out of the building. With every step, they give me tips on how to treat her and make her happy. I can hear them all the way to the exit.

I get to my place and dust a little. It isn't a big place. Everything is in the same room, except for the restroom. I clear everything on top of a small table for two next to my bed. I use it to place things on but never to eat. I clean the table and the kitchen. I don't have a lot of household items to use for cooking. I feel nervous. *Is this going to be enough for her to cook what she wants to? Is it good enough for her?* I have never bothered to think of stuff like this. I've never had to.

I finish quickly since there isn't much to clean. I arrange the table and take a shower. After that, I just sit on the side of my bed, waiting for her to arrive. Time seems to go slow. I feel impatient. I keep overthinking everything. I have arranged the plates and chairs at least a million times.

I hear a knock on the door. It is low and subtle. If I'd been making noise, I wouldn't have been able to hear it. I question if I really heard it or if my mind is playing tricks. I check just to be sure. I open the door.

There she is. The first things I notice are her eyes and her incredible smile. She is carrying a bag, and a guy stands behind her with two more. I find it weird. The guy hands me the bags and says goodbye to her. He seems serious and is taller than I am. I don't say anything. My face gives her clues that I have no idea what's going on. She walks in, and we unpack everything she has brought. She explains that her brother felt safer in sending her with an escort. I wonder if her brother just wants to know where I live, but I won't tell her that. I ask if the escort is going to wait for her. She looks at

ZETA

me awkwardly. I feel I've just made a mistake but don't know what it is.

She explains that it is already lights-out, and she isn't going all the way back in the middle of the night. I realize she is staying here with me. I smile. She can tell I am glad to hear that. My smile makes her smile. She instructs me to set everything up and help.

Not long after, she starts cooking, and I help with what I can. I have never cooked before. We talk and laugh the entire time. We make chicken with vegetables. She tells me the name of the recipe, but I am too distracted by her beauty to remember. We sit, and we eat slowly, taking our time, sharing stories and experiences. It is easy to talk to her. The conversation keeps going long after we finish eating. She keeps making me smile and laugh. I don't know what is happening with me. Everything around me seems to melt away. All I care about right now is spending time with her and making sure she enjoys being with me. I seem to have forgotten all the things inside myself that make me feel uneasy.

We finish eating, and we clean up everything. It is late now. I want to be respectful, and I tell her I will sleep on the floor. She tells me to get up and lie beside her. I lie there nervously, not knowing what to do. She turns around, facing the opposite direction. All I can do is stare at the ceiling. I can't go to sleep. Just being around her makes my heart race. In a moment, my brain stops thinking, and my body acts on its own. I turn toward her and wrap my hands around her. She grabs my hand, and we lie there cuddling. I don't get much sleep. I keep thinking of how great this moment is. I don't want to miss a second of it.

When the lights come on the next morning, I don't

VANTABLACK

feel tired at all. I feel happy, and I'm glad it wasn't a dream. We get up, and she cooks breakfast. I get ready for my day. When I am done, she smiles at me. I think she has been watching as I got ready. The table is set, and we are about to take a seat. We try walking past each other, but we bump into each other, I assume because of nervousness. She looks up at me. I have never been this close to her eyes and lips. She looks into my eyes, and we stand there for a moment. I grab her by the waist and press her body against mine. I reach out for her lips, and she does the same for mine. As we kiss, I can feel her passion with every movement. As my lips caress hers, I pull her closer with one hand and run the other one around her back. She places one hand on my cheek and the other one on my arm. Our kiss is so long the food is getting cold. She pulls away from me. She needs to catch her breath. Her eyes open slowly, looking at mine. She gives me a smile.

We finish eating, and I walk her toward the neutral zone. There, the same man who was with her last night, her escort, is waiting for us. I say goodbye to her. She leans forward to kiss me goodbye. I smile. This time, I can tell the smile is there, because it is a huge one. I stand there waiting for her to disappear into the distance. She has just left, and I am already eager to see her again.

I make my way into the Wolf building. I have to see if there is something I need to do and check to see if Miles needs anything from me.

When I enter the room, I see Eleonore leaving with some kids, heading to the building where she takes care of them and teaches them. We wave at each other from a distance. She says goodbye to Miles at the door, and

ZETA

Miles waits for me at the door while watching Eleonore go on her way. He is a man in love if ever I have seen one. I can't deny I am heading to that place myself.

We start catching up with each other about how things are going. He tells me the Tiger pack and Snake pack have been ordering more weapons, causing everyone else to buy more. That's good for us, yet we have to repair broken ones and gather metal. We have gotten some good deals with the other packs, which means more money for everyone and better rates on things we buy from other packs. It is going to be hard to balance spending time with Shanti and putting in time with the pack, since we have more things to do. I explain to Miles, and he agrees to put me in charge of a couple of guys. This is a huge deal. I have never been in charge of anyone. They will work, and I'll collect from them. Less hassle for me—I like that. It means I can spend more time with Shanti.

I don't see Shanti until two days later. I have been busy with the new arrangements of my position, so I haven't had the time. When I finally do see her, it is as if we just saw each other a few minutes before.

She smiles when she finds me staring. I always find myself amazed by her and the way she follows her heart. She knows what she wants, and even if everyone else tells her it is not the best choice, she prefers to find out rather than let others dictate her decisions. I am impressed that she has chosen me. It makes me feel good, as if she sees something in me I can't see. I feel fascinated by the way she lives. Everything she does is up to her.

She makes me feel as if she is not just with me but also my friend. I feel a freedom around her that I never

VANTABLACK

have felt before. She makes me forget about the metal walls that surround me in the bunker. I feel happiness and comfort. She adds value to my life. I wonder what I bring to the relationship we are developing. I ask her once during dinner after a couple of weeks of our being together.

"You don't judge me when I express myself," Shanti responds.

I wonder if that is enough for her. I never have noticed that. I always listen to her talk about her day or whatever is on her mind at the time. I just listen and give my opinions. I never tell her she is wrong for feeling or thinking the way she does. I am glad to hear I am not the only one feeling free.

Being with Shanti is a usual thing now. I invite her to stay when it gets too dark outside. Time flies by when we are together. Somehow, we never run out of things to talk about. I feel lucky to have encountered her on my path. Who would have known this hell hid someone toward whom I would grow to feel so dear?

Even on the worst days, such as when I have to go deliver to Julius once every week or two, her smile comforts me at the end of a long day. She never sees me as a monster for the things I do for the Wolf pack. Having a brother in the Fox pack might have normalized my way of life to her. Or she is falling for me so deeply that it blinds her to the devil I sometimes feel I am.

I can never do her wrong. I've never had someone care about me like she does. Growing up alone, I never knew what it was like to have someone else to care about. It made me oblivious to a lot of human emotions I saw others show toward one another but never really

ZETA

developed myself. Even in a place like this, I always felt like an outcast.

Now, having Shanti with me, I find feelings I have only heard others talk about and express. I have always heard people tell each other how much they care or how deeply they feel. To me, those were just words people said to create the illusion of caring for someone else, until Shanti began showing me the emotions behind those words. I feel she is the light shining in the darkness I have lived in my whole life. I am never able to find the words to tell her how grateful I am for her and to have her hold my hand and show me a life with color.

Even when I can't see her for a day or more, it is as if I am living a dream in which I am content and happy with my life. It is a first for me, and all the bad thoughts in my head stay away, out of sight. She is my dose of happiness and freedom. All she wants from me is my loyalty and honesty, and I deliver.

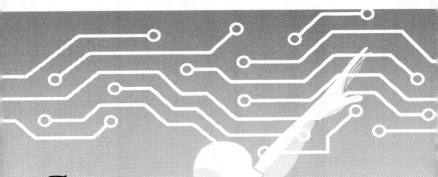

Seven

Eight months later

We have had the greatest months in the Wolf pack after the deals Miles made with the other packs. Everything is perfect. We get paid, and I have more time to spend with Shanti. She spends so much time at my place it is almost as if we live together. She made me ask her to date me after a while, and I happily obliged. It is a perfect world for us. We feel like kings. Things have run smoothly for the most part. Sometimes the delivery guys get beaten and robbed. We have to deliver either way. We keep our end of the bargains, slowly filling the terms of the agreements with each pack, delivering weapons at a steady rate, even when we face problems. It is like a dream. Unfortunately, dreams have to come to an end sometime.

ZETA

We have approximately one week until the weapons delivery commitments we have with the other packs come to an end. There are only so many weapons they can buy until they realize they don't need that many,

VANTABLACK

if they realize it. I make some deliveries myself from time to time to stay busy whenever I'm not spending time with Shanti. I go visit Marcus and Gilligan too whenever I'm not with Miles and the pack. I am busier than ever, and I'm fortunate enough to be able to handle everything.

Miles informs me of a delivery in the Fox zone. We are short on manpower, and I have time, so I decide to go. It is a big delivery, so Miles comes with me, and we make our way to their zone. It isn't a big package, but it's an important one, and we have no one else to back me up. It is the first time I have gone on a delivery with him. It's different. It's simpler. No problems come up, and no one follows us. We talk about how things are going. He asks about Shanti and me and how things are. We talk about plans and goals. It is a tough conversation since I haven't thought about any of that since I've been with her. I don't know how to answer him. It takes me a while to think about the answer.

Finally, I tell him I want to make enough money not to have to worry about having to eat. That's something no one has been able to do yet. I want to be the first one to have all the time in the world, even if it is inside this bunker. I want to spend my days with Shanti and help her help others. Maybe helping everyone is the way to make it out of here. Fixing the bunker may mean everyone will have time to try to fix the world out there. How can you fix the world when you can't even fix your health or eating situation?

He smiles, and I think he understands. I'm glad he doesn't try to persuade me to do otherwise. He says he had that same goal a long time ago, but life steered him in a different direction. His dream didn't last long. In the

ZETA

end, he doesn't try to change my mind. He is willing to let me figure it out by myself. He says only that I am not the first hopeful person in this place. It doesn't sound like a person killing a dream, more like fueling it. I feel he believes in me, even if I fail. He always makes me feel there is no way I can fail at what I try, and even if I do, I can get back up and try again if I want.

We keep talking all the way to the drop-off zone. We arrive at the Fox building. It has some graffiti outside, so it isn't hard to identify. The leader of the Fox pack is waiting for us outside, smoking a cigarette with his right-hand man, Zack, Shanti's brother. They are sharing the cigarette as they have a conversation in the street. They see us walking toward them and keep talking without a care in the world. They are patient, it seems; we are still far away, and they don't seem to care. When we get close enough, Miles asks me for the package. I hand it over to him. I can't see them that clearly from so far behind, but I can see them enough to know it is them.

The leader of the Fox pack is a tall man older than Miles, with gray-and-black hair. For someone as old as he is, he is in pretty good shape. Judging by the scars on his right arm, which run along all the way to his fingers, he is a fighter. I have seen some scars like his on Miles, Gilligan, and Marcus from time to time. They seem deep.

The men smile at each other and hug like old friends. Miles follows him inside the building, asking me to stay outside.

Zack, Shanti's brother, waits outside with me. He wears an orange jacket with black stripes and designs on it and a white shirt under it. If I hadn't known ahead of time, I would never have known he is related to her.

VANTABLACK

He doesn't say anything for a while. Finally, when I decide to sit down and rest, he decides to give me a piece of his mind.

"So you are the one who has been dating my sister?" It sounds like a question, but I know he isn't looking for an answer. "She has a liking for you. I haven't seen her this happy in a very long time. When she comes back from spending time with you, she can't seem to stop smiling. I'm glad for that, and I thank you for it."

I look up and notice he isn't even looking at me. He is facing the same way I am.

"I'm glad she has found a way to enjoy herself. That said, you understand that if something was to happen to her, I would come for you. Her guard already told me where to find you."

I get back on my feet calmly and step shoulder to shoulder with him. "I could never hurt someone who makes me feel like she does. I'm with her until the moment she doesn't want me around anymore," I say in a calm voice.

Half a smile appears on his face. "I know you dogs are loyal; that's not my issue. What I'm saying is, if anything happens while she is with you, I don't care if you end up losing your life, but Shanti better be fine by the end of it. I take care of her when she is with me. I don't need to be stressing about whether she is going to be okay with you."

I understand his concern. It isn't a peaceful life we live, and he is asking me to keep my shit separate from her. If I'm not able to do so, I at least have to make sure the flames don't reach her. "No need for stressing. Nothing can touch her as long as I'm around."

He smiles, pulls out a pack of cigarettes, and offers

ZETA

me one. I deny. He lights up one for himself, and we keep watching ahead of us. He has made it clear what he expects from me, and I respect that. It's not easy to ask another person to take care of someone you hold dear. To do it, you have to be able to lower the walls built around your heart in this type of life. Those moments are the ones I try to focus on more than the bad ones. I find them more meaningful.

After a while, Miles comes out, saying goodbye to the leader. I nod at him and then turn to Zack. I look him in the eye and nod at him also. Miles shakes Zack's hand, and we start walking again, this time in a different direction.

We make our way to the Snake zone. Since the two territories are close to each other, we might as well go. Miles has some business to discuss with their leader. I haven't seen him, but I know his name: Kristov. He is known for trying to push on other territories from time to time. Sometimes he is able to hold them for a long time. Others times, he loses a lot of men by trying. Out of all the leaders, he is one of the most feared. Everyone thinks he is crazy. He always makes decisions without thinking. He is erratic. Half the bunker fear Julius from the Tiger pack for his way of handling things, but everyone knows he thinks things through. He is malevolent and smart. The other half fear Kristov because he is vile and erratic. The way his mind works makes everyone always be on the lookout for his actions, especially the Elephant pack since they have to put out his fires.

Now we are heading toward Kristov. He has asked Miles for a meeting without specifying the reason or giving details. I'm worried he might try something while

VANTABLACK

we are there. If this thought has crossed my mind, I'm sure it has also crossed his. Miles is never nervous. He always seems in control of himself, despite what's going on around him. I can't imagine the kind of pressure he must go through to be this calm when walking into the mouth of the snake.

We knock on the door. Oddly, no one is at the entrance of the building. Most packs always have someone covering their headquarters. The door opens slowly. A man takes one look at Miles and opens the door with a big, creepy smile. I assume everyone in the Snake pack is as crazy as Kristov. The place is a mess, and all the doors to the rooms seem to have been broken down. We follow the man to a big open room in the middle of the building. Kristov is standing there with his hands extended to his sides, facing upward, with his back turned to us. When we get close enough to Kristov, the man disappears into the darkness, leaving us three.

Miles clears his throat to let him know we are here. Kristov turns around slowly. Aside from being crazy, he is also known for his love of drama and theatrics. His smile is disturbingly long, and his mouth is wider than the average person's.

"Miles, my boy, how are you?" he asks, slowly approaching Miles for a hug.

Miles smiles at him. He is calm like undisturbed water. On the other hand, I'm on edge, trying my best to hold it together. I keep expecting him to do something insane with every second that elapses.

With a soft and calm voice, Miles answers, "Kristov, what can I do you for?"

He pats Miles on the shoulders and smiles at him as he stares. He stands there for a second, holding him by

ZETA

the shoulders, like a statue. The only thing that moves is his smile, which shifts from a friendly smile to a diabolical one.

Quietly, I hold my breath. Kristov instantly changes his gaze toward me. He hasn't noticed me until this moment. As if waking from a trance, he is back in the room with us. I guess I wasn't as silent as I thought.

"We are in a hurry right now, Kris. What did you want to talk about?" Miles says, getting his attention again.

Kristov smiles. "I was wondering if you could get some things for me. I need them in large quantities, and I assume you are the man for the job. If I'm wrong, I would appreciate you pointing me to the right person."

"That depends on what you need me to get for you. How much, and how often?" Miles says, trying to hurry the conversation along.

"I need some motherboards. A lot of them. Thirty-five of them. All of them delivered in seven days or less. What do you say, Miles? Are your dogs up for the task?" Kristov says as he turns his gaze in my direction.

"Sure. We expect payment before each one is delivered."

"Excellent. I didn't expect any less from the wonder boy Miles. After all, that's why you were chosen to lead the doggy pack, right?" Kristov answers. It is clear they know each other from way back, and he is trying to use something from the past to make Miles react.

Miles nods and gives Kristov a smile. Kristov extends a hand, and they shake on it. They look into each other's eyes. Kristov seems to want to hold on to Miles's hand with anger. Miles remains calm. He takes a step closer

VANTABLACK

to Kristov, who gets the message and releases his hand from his grip. Miles starts to walk away, and I follow.

"Next time you want a delivery of some sort, don't make me come all the way over here for something we could have taken care of the normal way," Miles says to Kristov as we walk away, without turning back to look at him. I can't help myself; I look back for a second. Kristov smiles at Miles and stands there until we leave the building. I can't shake the feeling there is a lot of history between them.

After we make it back to the Wolf building, we are about to say our goodbyes.

"By the way, I'm going to need you in the upcoming days. I'll be sending some men to take care of Kristov's order. That means I'll need you to do some deliveries to Julius. He must have had a liking after that first delivery. He asked for you specifically," Miles says as he opens the door.

I stand on the street, processing what he is telling me. It is odd to me that Julius wants me to do more deliveries for him. We are about to finish with the big batch of weapons he ordered.

"I guess he wants to finish smoothly without setbacks. Right?" I say.

"I guess so. Either way, we are about to complete all the orders we had. All we have to do is finish strong. Finish delivering the last weapons to each group and the motherboards to Kristov. After that, everything will be back to normal. My best guess is the Tigers and Snakes are about to go to war over a few blocks. If that happens, they will be asking for more orders, depending on how things go. Either way, Julius wants you to deliver his packages from now on. He has been complaining about

ZETA

the other guys, since they don't make it sometimes. The last packages are very important. He must trust you to deliver them, since he has never asked for anyone before."

It seems odd, but I feel more at peace delivering to Julius than having to see Kristov every day for a week. I simply nod at him.

"Go home, and get some rest. We have a long day tomorrow." He smiles.

I make my way home. I know Shanti is already waiting for me. She has been cooking for me a lot since she started staying with me, which is great, especially today, since I haven't eaten all day. I am starving.

When I open the door, she is serving dinner. It smells delicious. I make my way toward her as she sets everything in place. I interrupt her and give her a kiss. She smiles at me.

"Did you miss me that much?" she asks as she pours us lemonade to accompany our meal.

I give her a smile as an answer. We eat and start a conversation about our day. I don't mention meeting her brother or what we said. I focus the conversation on her. I don't want to talk about meeting Kristov or future wars between packs that might or might not happen. I ask her about her day and try to stay on that topic.

She talks about giving food out to some people down on their luck. She also helped some mothers and elderly persons with chores. She is tired after all that. It doesn't matter how many times we talk about her day, every time she tells me about helping others, I can hear the pride and joy in her voice. She seriously believes that one day, she will be done, and this place will be better for everyone. I'm not so sure, but I believe in

VANTABLACK

her and her passion for helping others. That is enough for me to be on board with her personal quest. Some days she speaks with such passion and emotion that I believe she is close to turning people's lives around for the better. I never discourage her or make her feel as if she is wasting her time. She always comes back with a smile, even after a bad day. The light in her eyes never goes away. I love sitting with her and talking about how she helps others and her future goals and plans. It is something uncommon around here. We keep talking long after we finish eating. When we notice the time, we go to sleep, and we'll start all over tomorrow. It's enough for me.

As usual, I wake up holding her hand. We get up and have breakfast. She gets out of bed just to eat with me and talk some more, even though we had dinner together last night. As soon as we see the lights come on outside, she kisses me as I walk toward the door. We say our goodbyes, and I leave her there to get ready for her day. I make my way toward the Wolf building to get the package I need to deliver. I have never had a feeling like this before. I used to have routines that felt forced or didn't have a point, but with Shanti, everything is better. I find myself complaining less, if at all, about this bunker, which I can see now is protecting us. It's incredible how one person can change your point of view, like adding color to a gray world.

Eight

I collect the weapons to be delivered today and make my way. No one is following me, as groups did the first time. It is pretty easy; it almost seems as if no one wants what I am carrying. Since all the packs are ordering weapons from us now, I guess they're all trying to protect what they have or what is coming their way.

I reach the Tiger building, ready to deliver. I extend my hand to the doorman to give him the package, but he refuses to accept it. He opens the door and signals for me to go inside. It feels unnecessary, but I understand. Each pack has their way of doing things. Some, such as the Ape pack, don't even let you inside. I have never been to their zone, but I have heard from the other guys that the Apes intercept anyone at least five streets from the building.

I follow the corridor to the room I've made past deliveries to. Julius is waiting for me with the same guy he was with last time. The guy is now missing half his arm. I glance at it without anyone noticing. I don't want to ask what happened, and I don't want to be caught staring.

The interaction goes smoothly—no demonstrations or theatrics like the first time. I just deliver the package, and he smiles and thanks me. Everyone is happy to

VANTABLACK

get the deliveries, and we are just happy to be getting paid. Everyone goes on his way after each delivery. The thought of just finishing the week keeps popping up in my head like a bell every few hours. I guess things are going to be slow after that, and I'm going to have more free time like before. I can't wait to go visit Marcus and Gilligan again to see what they have been up to. *Just finish the week, and everything will be back to being slow and peaceful.*

I keep going day after day. Each day is easier than before. I complete smooth deliveries, and I have good, pleasant times when I'm not working for the Wolves. In the blink of an eye, the last day of deliveries arrives. It is back to dealing in small quantities and seeing what we have to get our hands on to trade and deliver. We've made a killing, and it is hard not to spend it. I save as much as I can and treat myself and Shanti at the same time.

As I walk to make my last delivery, I know things are changing. In my head, they are going back to how everything was before, only now I have more money. I don't know how wrong I am. Everyone's world is about to change for the worse, and we are all unaware—like being asleep one moment and waking up surrounded by fire, with no way out of the room.

I make it to the Tiger building. The doorman isn't there. I knock on the door several times without an answer. I wait and wait, but no one shows up. I go around the building, hoping to find someone. When I head back to the front, the door is open halfway. I walk toward it and yell to see if anyone is inside. I already know where to deliver the package, so I walk to the room where I always meet Julius. With every step, my

ZETA

mind keeps telling me this situation is a setup. But I ignore my gut and keep going.

I place the package on the table once I make it to the room. As I'm about to walk out, Julius enters the room. His clothes have blood on them, and so does part of his face. The man who usually follows him isn't around this time. I assume the worst and think the blood is his. There is no way to know for sure.

"Thanks for being so reliable with the deliveries. I like consistency in my work, and I knew you could give me that. There's something about knowing how things will play out that makes me feel at ease. I suppose we all feel that way, huh?" He checks the delivery and then walks toward me. I'm still at the exit of the room.

I can't shake the feeling that there is something wrong about this whole situation. I just fake a smile and nod at him. I don't want to make the conversation longer and spend any more time here than I need to.

"Here you go, kid. As a token of my appreciation for not missing a step with my valuables." He pulls out a necklace.

It is beautiful—a shade of red I haven't seen before. I feel it is a bad idea to accept it, but before I can say no, he places it in my hand.

"Keep it close to you at all times." He gives me a smile. "Now I have to go back to my schedule." He shows me to the exit and closes the door behind me.

I place the necklace in my pocket and make my way to Shanti, who is waiting for me. It is getting late, and the Tiger pack is the last delivery I have to do. I am meeting her in the Fox zone. Since the Fox zone is in the middle of the Tiger and Snake zones, I figured after my last delivery, I would walk back home with her.

VANTABLACK

As I make my way to her, I pull out the necklace. It has an enchanting, beautiful color. I can tell it is very old, maybe even older than the bunker. I have never seen a rock so beautiful. I want to give it to Shanti. *It doesn't matter where it came from*, I think. *An object can't be malevolent or evil. It's just an object.* The thoughts in my head start making sense, especially since there is no ill intent. I will give her the necklace when I see her. I place it in my pocket for the time being. After I do, I feel something weird on my hand. There is blood on it. Julius must have smeared some on it when he handed it to me. I wipe my hand as best as I can. I don't want Shanti to see it.

I arrive at the Fox building. Shanti is outside, saying goodbye to her brother. I've made it in time. Zack and I say hello and then goodbye. They seem to have had a pleasant day. Shanti and I start walking back home. Zack stays outside to smoke a cigarette. I ask Shanti about her day as we walk. Everything is going great for her too, and that's all I can ask for. A couple of streets later, I stop her.

I pull out the necklace and show it to her. I can tell from her face that she also thinks it is beautiful. I place it around her neck. She admires it for a second. I can see, in the distance, Zack still smoking a cigarette, looking at us. Shanti kisses me and holds my hand. We continue our long walk home. As we make our way, people are clearing the streets. When people turn to look at us, they can't help but take a look at Shanti and the necklace. I don't mind it. It is a beautiful necklace being worn by the most beautiful soul I have had the luck to meet. I assume it has caught them off guard. There aren't many accessories worn here. I think the

87

ZETA

only person I have seen with one is Eleonore. She has a blue rock on her necklace. It is covered most of the time by her clothing. Miles gave it to her. I figure it's the thing to do, so I've given my necklace to the person I love, just as Miles did. She keeps turning heads all the way to the room.

We arrive and finish our day as we usually do. I think maybe this is something everyone goes through: people hate this place until they find someone to be with who shows them maybe it's not as bad as they think. I know I don't deserve her love, but I am grateful for it. Shanti is my love.

The next day, we wake up to a knock on the door before the lights come on outside. The knocks intensify as I rush to the door. I open it. Shanti is sitting in bed, covering herself. It is Miles with Gilligan and Marcus. They are covered in sweat, as if they've run all the way here. Miles pushes the door open, and they all make their way inside.

"What happened?" Miles asks. He turns to look at Shanti and notices the necklace.

"Oh fuck," Gilligan says as he brushes his hair back with both hands.

I have no idea what is going on. I ask, but they don't give me an answer yet.

"Where did you get the necklace?" Marcus asks.

I explain how Julius gave it to me after the delivery as a gift, and I gave it to Shanti. They believe me without a shadow of doubt. I have never given them a reason not to trust me.

"That belonged to Julius's girlfriend," Miles says. "He told the Elephant militia he found her dead. He told

VANTABLACK

them you were the last person to be with her. They are on their way here to get you."

I can't believe what I am hearing.

"They heard from some people in the streets that you were seen showing off the necklace as you walked down the street yesterday."

I realize people's heads turned not because Shanti looked beautiful in the necklace but because everyone knew whom it belonged to. I am the only one who had no idea. My gut was trying to save me, and I ignored it. It was a setup after all.

"Julius wants your head delivered. We can't keep you safe. I'm sorry."

Miles's words sink deep in my chest. I have been on this path for so long, and I still don't know the rules.

I ask Miles why. He takes a second to answer. I have never seen him like this. Usually, he is always under control, no matter the situation.

"If we don't turn you in, that means a war against the Tiger pack and against the Elephants. Aside from that, they are screaming that they want justice. If we turn you in, you are dead. We need to find a place for you to lie low," Miles says.

"Miles—"

Miles cuts Marcus off. "No one can know where you are, not even us. You are going to have to find a place to hide fast and to stay low for a long time. Maybe some of the other levels in the bunker. The packs only have strength in this level. As long as you keep moving from time to time, they won't be able to find you." He talks as he packs some things for me to take.

Gilligan tries to get a word in. "Miles, if he leaves—"

"I know!" Miles yells in frustration.

89

ZETA

I question him. I want to know what they have to say. Miles doesn't let them. He tells me to say my goodbyes to Shanti. She removes the necklace and places it in my hand. I am at the door. They are all watching me. I kiss her.

"I'm going to fix this," I say, trying to give them comfort.

"Just stay alive, and stay away long enough for all of this to blow over. Then you will be able to come back," Miles says, pushing me out the door with some hope. I believe in his words.

I start running. Behind me, I can hear the commotion of the Tiger pack and the Elephant pack searching for me. I have to make my way toward the hole in the wall. My heart is beating so hard I feel as if it's coming out of my chest. I run, crossing streets and evading everyone. Most of the people I encounter are Vultures, but they don't care about anything. There is no reward for turning anyone in.

After running for a long time, I finally make it to the wall. The hole is gone. My safe haven has been cut off from me. I haven't been to it in so long that I have no idea when the repairs happened. But I know I have to come up with a new plan—and quick. I have no idea what I am feeling. I have no time to processes anything, not even my thoughts. I feel anger and then sadness. *Left turn. Right turn.* I feel fear and paranoia. *Upper levels or lower ones?* I am running on adrenaline. Every decision is made from impulse. Instinct is the only thing I rely on right now. I can't stop to take a minute to think. They might catch up. I make my way toward the lower levels.

Shanti, my life, and everything I have that makes

VANTABLACK

me happy are being taken away from me. There is nothing I can do. One second, I lay in bed, feeling lucky to have her, and the next, Julius took everything without even breaking a sweat. Each step puts me farther away from them. Loneliness surrounds me. I try not to be afraid, but it is hard not to be when I am being hunted. I keep going down lower and lower without being seen, until I reach the last level.

There is hardly any light. The last level is where all the waste comes, and they recycle it to be able to grow crops. It smells horrible. Trash and human waste are thrown in here among bodies of the dead and everything else no one wants. I guess it's just the place for me now, given the situation. Workers separate everything into piles for anything that can be reused, and whatever can't be recycled is broken down.

I make my way into the darkness. I find an area where I can stop to think now that I am far from the grasp of my pursuers. I feel horrible about leaving everyone like this, but I have no choice. I take a moment to deal with my feelings before moving on to my thoughts. I need to deal with what I am feeling inside first. After that, I will have to think of what I should do now that this is my home. What am I going to eat? How will I live?

The people who work on this level start to show up for their shift. Some of them see me and ignore me. Everyone goes about his business as my world shatters all around me. It's incredible how the world doesn't skip a beat, even when it feels as if you've reached the end.

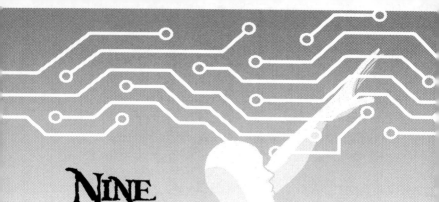

Nine

I do my best to control my feelings. The darkness around me hides me well, surrounding me with its embrace, hiding the parts of me that are breaking down. Slowly, I start to feel at home, as if I deserve this for some reason. It doesn't take long for my thoughts to turn on me and highlight why this is the last stop of my journey. The hours pass by, and I have nothing to do but focus on what I am going through and how I can get out. Every plan hits the same dead end. I know there is no way I am getting out of this hole. The moments that make me smile start to distance themselves from me. I don't eat today. My body is asking for nourishment, but my mind is away, paralyzing my body, escaping the darkness merging with my heart and soul like a virus taking over. Is this life's way of telling me I chose the wrong path? Life gave me peace and happiness only to drag me from it when my guard was down.

Anger starts to take over. The anger merges with hate and revenge. The darkness around me merges every bad feeling, binding them all together with its magnetic pull like hands collecting everything that shouldn't be in a person's heart and allowing it to become a major part of it, allowing my anger and lust for justice to form a dagger to save me from the place I find myself in. I

VANTABLACK

have never found myself going through thoughts like I do today, but the darkness keeps whispering in my ear that each one was rightfully earned. I fall asleep with the most ill-hearted and nefarious thoughts my head can come up with. The floor is cold and covered in filth, but the darkness slowly approaches me as my eyes try to stay open. She extends her hand and offers warmth for the night if she can find shelter in my head and heart. I allow her to come in without a second thought. All I want is to feel good, even if only for a second. It doesn't matter if the price is a piece of what makes me who I am so proud to be.

As my eyes close, I find heat inside myself next to the place where the darkness has decided to rest. I can feel it. She lights a fire to keep herself warm. Selfish, she has done it only for herself, like all her actions, but since she is resting in my heart for the night, the heat reaches me as well. Something demonic is extending inside me like an animal waking up and stretching. This darkness has awakened something that not even I knew lived inside. As I drift away, I have my last thought: *If the world is going to give me the worst it has to offer and drag me to hell, I'll become the demon the world fears but has yet to meet.*

ZETA

My eyes open. The hunger and pain in my stomach wake me. I spent the previous day dealing with myself and didn't eat. Now I am paying for it. I can't go back into the upper levels; there's too much light there, and I am still being hunted. I do the only thing I can think of: I wander around this level, looking for something to eat in the cold, dark piles of trash and waste. There is nothing. Everyone above me is as hungry as I am. They don't waste anything. If something is down here on this

VANTABLACK

level, it means that everything it had to give was already removed from it.

As the day passes, the hunger in my stomach turns into pain. Toward the end of the day, the pain fuels my rage. The noise around me in every direction amplifies. My stomach isn't grumbling anymore; it just goes ahead and starts digesting my body, as if it knows I have nothing to give. The hunger pains are impossible to ignore. I keep walking around the place, hoping to find something that isn't here. I hope maybe I'll find an animal lurking, and then I will have to do the unthinkable. But I know in my heart that I won't find animals all the way down here. The whole place reeks of chemicals. No animal could make its way down here, even if there was a plate set out for it to eat the most delicious meal imaginable.

I keep going even after my legs and stomach beg me to stop. I keep thinking maybe I am close to finding something. I have to keep convincing myself that maybe if I search a little more, food will be waiting for me, hidden somewhere. I never find it. The thirst and hunger make my head pound and hurt me. I finally give up and lie facedown on the floor. Not long after, I drift into my memories. I keep coming and going from my head to reality. It's the second day, and it feels like an eternity. No time for hatred today.

I dream of drinking the lemonade Shanti made back in our place. She always knew exactly how much sugar to put in to make it to my liking. I grab the glass and drink it as fast as I can. I start coughing. I am drinking out of a puddle where my face lies. Water and chemicals make their way down into my stomach but not for long. The pain in my stomach intensifies, and

Z E T A

what I have swallowed comes out again. I am losing myself. How can I go back up, when I don't even have time to think about how to reclaim my life? As I lie here facing upward, with puke coming out of my stomach, I swear the world is against me. Enough to torture me and drive me mad but never fully get rid of me. My only friend is the darkness, which brings me hallucinations of fears I don't know I have, making me feel alive again, just like the memories of times spent with my loved ones. She likes to play with me. If I am strong enough to go through all the fear, I am rewarded with a memory that makes me happy. Those are her rules. Next thing I know, I am waiting anxiously for the next hallucination with the worst fear she has to give.

The days keep going as everything is broken down around me as well as inside, as if I am falling without a way to grab on to something. I don't know how many days have passed after the third one. It doesn't matter anymore. After a while, I lose myself, and the darkness delivers the version of me she wants. Sometimes I can't remember why I am down here or how I got to this place. The chemicals in the air exaggerate the speed with which I am losing myself. The days sometimes feel like one constant day, and other times, I feel as if I have been here for years. I swear the fumes of the chemicals make me spiral down faster. Other times, the fumes make me feel as if they've fed me just enough to live another minute. They enhance my torment, and other times, they make me numb to it all. What a depressing existence. I start to scream to myself, thinking of new ways to end it all from time to time. The longer I am down here, the further I walk from the person I was.

I drift in and out of the labyrinth inside my head,

VANTABLACK

going insane, trying to find a way out. The time I spend inside my head seems to last forever. Time runs slower here.

Another hallucination starts. I move and talk, but my body never leaves the ground it lies on.

I am in a sea of darkness, trying to stay above the water as the waves take me where they want to. It's never a clear destination. I finally land on a metallic beach. I start walking toward a city not far from where I stand. As I walk toward it, the water turns into metal and disappears, becoming part of the floor. The more I walk, the farther away the city seems to be. I grow tired and stop. I look back to see if it's too late to return to the beach. Everything is gone. The floor all around me is made of concrete, and walls start to rise out of the metal. I am back in the bunker. I walk the empty streets. The buildings that have just formed begin to shake, collapsing one after the other.

A giant tiger walks among them, pushing them with its body, causing them to fall. The tiger has a snake wrapped around its neck like a necklace. It approaches me, but it doesn't do anything but stare and walk around me. It finally stops in front of me. I don't feel fear. Finally, it attacks me, with its paws scratching my stomach. My organs fall onto the floor as I collapse to my knees. The tiger just looks at me as if waiting for me to do something regarding its actions. I look down as the blood escapes my body rapidly. As I try to look up, the snake bites me in the neck, poisoning me. The tiger and snake take a final look before walking back to where they came from. I don't feel pain. The buildings they dropped start to burn as they walk closer to them. I can see the tiger walking away, heading toward Shanti.

ZETA

She stands there surrounded by debris and flames. She has nowhere to go.

I can feel my heart still beating as it falls onto the floor with the rest of my organs. It beats faster and faster as the tiger and the snake approach Shanti. I see the tiger raise a paw, showing its claws to Shanti.

"Stop." That's all I can gather the energy to say.

The tiger attacks her, and the snake bites her. She lies on the floor dying, with her eyes looking at me. She gives me a smile as she leaves this world.

My heart stops beating, and I feel anger and rage. I want vengeance and justice. As the anger in me flows, I feel a warmth around me. My body starts to regenerate as my blood flows back into my body. The tiger begins to walk backward. It is facing Shanti again, and she gets back up. I see everything play back in reverse. The tiger walks toward me. I have the strength to stand again. I look down, and my body is back, except for my heart. It's still beating on the floor. I look up, and the tiger has its claws up, waiting to take a swing at me. When it does, I see confusion in its eyes. Its paw is on the other side of me now. It has missed, but I haven't moved. I take a step toward the tiger, and the snake attacks. It bites me, but its mouth starts to wither away, expanding to its body. The tiger drops it as the snake becomes ash and dies slowly and painfully. The tiger takes another swing, and its paw goes flying. It is injured and can't run away. I keep walking toward it as it drags itself away in a cowardly manner. The tiger can see it in my eyes: I am gone. It finally moves out of the way as I walk toward Shanti. I forget all about the tiger as it goes into hiding in the darkness.

I hold Shanti close, and all the rage and anger

VANTABLACK

disappear. I collapse onto the floor, unable to live without a heart. Shanti holds me close as I take my last breath and die peacefully in her hands.

I come back from my mind in flashes. My face is lying in a puddle of water and chemicals. My face has turned red, as the chemicals have given it a rash. I lie there as time passes me by. The workers come and go. Going on with their lives, they avoid me or don't even notice me. I can't tell.

I wake up at some point from my darkest trips into the darkness that consumes my heart and mind. A man is pouring water into my mouth. I drink as I struggle to get enough. I wonder why he is helping me. I think he must be confusing me with one of the workers here. Maybe he thinks I got dehydrated from overworking and came to my aid. I have no strength to question him. I have barely enough strength to drink the water. He stays with me until I finish the cup he has brought me. I can tell he is a patient man.

As I drink, I hear a commotion.

"Look in every corner!" a strange shadow hollers at another.

I know my pursuers are here for me. They probably searched all the other levels until they reached this one. They look at all the workers and examine the areas where all the waste is piled up, carefully avoiding getting any of it on themselves. One of them makes his way toward us. As he approaches, his steps become louder. I know in my heart this is this end. I try to make my peace with it.

"What happened to him?" the shadow asks the man helping me.

As I hear the words, I can't help but grip on to the

ZETA

man helping me. My hand holds his wrist. I am too weak, and my body reacts to the fear of meeting my doom. I grip his wrist for a second. I guess he notices.

"We were working, and when I turned around, he collapsed. Dehydration. He fell face-first into this here puddle of chemicals we use to clean. When I saw him go down, I came to his aid," the man with the helping hand says.

Why would he lie for me? Or does he think this is the truth? I can't tell.

When the shadow hears the words *puddle* and *chemicals*, he takes a step back. From a distance, he tries to take a look at me. The darkness surrounding us doesn't let him see well enough. He walks away and keeps looking elsewhere before taking his men with him.

I want to ask the man why he helped me. Why risk himself for someone he has never met? If only I had enough strength to make a sound. All my strength is going into my hand to guide this stranger as he pours water into my decaying body. I finish the cup, and the man helps me off my back. He sits me up against something. Without saying anything, he leaves. My eyes try to follow him as he walks away, but it is hard to keep them open. I am passing out. I keep trying to yell or scream to call him back, but I can't get a sound out. I try to raise my hand, but there is no use. He walks away back to his doings. I drifted back into the nightmare inside my head. The darkness is calling me back.

When I regain consciousness, I feel slightly better. I'm not as gone as before. I don't know how long I have lain here, but I have some strength in me now. It isn't a lot, but it is enough to move around. Everything hurts,

VANTABLACK

but I know now I can't just lie here dying slowly. My thoughts start to make sense to me more than before. Slowly, I'm regaining part of myself. I know that what I have gone through here is going to be part of it too.

I walk around looking for food again. Some workers have brought food to eat down here. They see me stare from the shadows. One of them calls to me. I walk over. He gives me part of his food. He lets me sit down next to him, and they keep going with their conversation. I can't help the tears running silently down my face. I eat as I try to cover them. If only I could ask why they are doing this for me.

They finish eating and get back up to go finish their shift. Most of them have leftovers, and they all give the extra food to me as I sit here still eating. No one says anything. They just give me food and leave back to their business, as if it is not a big deal. I eat everything slowly, as I am having trouble with my body taking in food. I will stay here as long as it takes; I am going to finish every bit they have given me. Even though my stomach feels full because it has shrunk from not eating, I will finish it.

They all finish their shift, and I'm still sitting here, finishing up what they gave me. As soon as I am done, I lie on the ground and get some sleep.

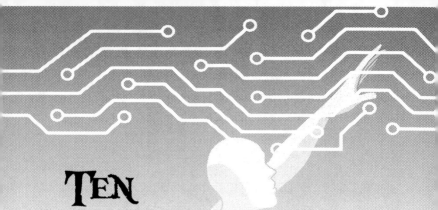

Ten

A huge tremble in the ground wakes me up in the middle of my sleep. Then comes another tremble and another after that. I have no idea what is happening. The whole ground is shaking. It doesn't last long, and then there is silence. Everything stops. I don't think much of it and lie back to sleep again. I need to rest for now. I have to come back to my senses and regain as much strength as I can.

When I wake up, the fumes and all the noise are gone. The piles of debris and waste aren't falling anymore. I walk around for hours. The workers don't show up today. Everything stands still. I have recovered some of my energy, thanks to the food the men shared with me. I am grateful. I wait for them to show up, so I can thank them, but no one comes. I walk all over the place, as I did when I first came down here. I need to think of my next move now that I have enough strength to think clearly. I'm glad the fumes are dying down, and things make sense. I can't do anything about how dark it is, but I am just glad my thoughts are starting to be my own again. I have nothing to do, and sitting still makes the time go by slower. I walk when I need to think and sleep when my body screams for food. That is my temporary solution for now.

VANTABLACK

The complete absence of noise and chaos helps me gather my thoughts. The chemicals don't torment me anymore now that they are almost nonexistent. I think it is odd that not even one thing has dropped down like before. I wonder what has happened, but there is no way to know. My attention keeps diverting from place to place, but I can feel it becoming clearer as time elapses. It is just a matter of when I will be able to be myself again completely. I allow myself to wander freely and let my thoughts roam free. I know that everything inside me is trying to recover. I can't do anything to speed up the process, so it's up to my body and mind to let me know when they are ready to get out of the darkness. I rest some more as I gather the pieces of what this place has made of me.

It is the second day of silence. Again, no one comes down to this level to work. I wonder what's happening. I am beginning to worry. I make my way to the closest stairway to go back up. I can't remember which way I came from, and I have no idea what territory I will come out in when I reach the pack level. I have to be careful. I cover my head and part of my face as a precaution, not that I need to. My face is clearing slowly from the rash from the chemicals. The filth that covers me makes me unrecognizable.

As I make my way to the stairs, I hear something falling and then a loud noise. It isn't far from me. It lands among the piles of debris and waste. As it rolls down, I know what it is: a dead body. I wonder what happened. This isn't the way bodies are disposed of. I look toward the stairs, thinking maybe someone will come running down after the mistake he made, but nobody comes. I look up, and then it happens: body after body falls from

ZETA

every hole in the ceiling of this level. Some are burned, and the odor mixes with the stench of what is already down here. Others have been killed and mutilated. Dead people are all around me. There are bodies of all ages on the piles that continue to form.

A cold feeling crawls down my spine, but it isn't because of the bodies. It's because I notice I'm not surprised or scared at what is happening. I feel nothing at the moment. I'm numb. Maybe I'm curious about how the bodies found their way here, but I feel no fear or sadness. I know this place has changed me.

I am at the bottom of the stairs, looking up. I place a hand in front of me, trying to cover my eyes from all the light. I have been in the darkness so long that the light is blinding. I look down as I take a step and then another and another. Slowly, my body climbs the stairs one by one. I have recovered, but I still find it difficult to climb up.

As I take each step, I feel a change. I can feel my mind reverting. The labyrinth in my head starts to dissipate. The chemicals that once gave my fear and rage claws and form have no weight over me now. I can't shake the scars I feel in my soul after what I have experienced here. I can't rid myself of the part that has fought the insanity of being in this place. To be honest, I don't know if I can't or if I don't want to do it. I feel I need part of that if I am going to come back to everyone and stay alive. I have to prepare for what I need to do. I have to clear my name, and I know there is no peaceful way of doing it. So here I am, climbing up slowly. I wonder if Julius can hear the steps. Can he sense the animal crawling out of his lair to eat?

My eyes adapt to the light after a while. I have several

104

VANTABLACK

levels to go up before reaching my destination. I have to go through the worker levels, among other kinds, to reach where the packs live. The whole way there, I feel as if I am in a dream. Not a single person is in sight. I walk toward a tree on my path. I take some apples from it and eat them as I walk without stopping. I can't waste time. I need to make it soon. I don't know when I will start encountering people. I don't want to get handed over to Julius, as that would ruin everything for me.

I walk level after level and finally make it to the one I need to be on. I am tired, and my legs are aching. I can feel my muscles burning. As I make my way up the stairs, I see smoke dying down from destroyed buildings. The buildings that were once here are mostly torn down. There are flames still burning on others. No one is around. I walk through the streets, trying to figure out which territory I am in. I walk in one direction, searching for something to give me an idea, but everything is unrecognizable.

I feel as if I've walked into another nightmare. Everything I once knew is destroyed. Far away on the street I walk on, I see people. I keep walking in the same direction to avoid suspicion. As I get closer, I see what they are doing: picking bodies from the street. Some are burned, and others are unrecognizable. They won't notice me unless I run at them on fire. They are moving the dead to clear the streets. Others are moving rocks and debris to clear a path. Everyone who is helping is beat and tired; their hands are covered in blood or red from burns from picking up the rocks—it's hard to tell.

I walk like a ghost. I notice everything happening around me. The others have no time to notice anything

ZETA

at all. There are no injured. Some of the dead have stab wounds, or they were cut until they bled out.

I wonder how all this came to be in my absence. My thoughts are cut short when I hear a man behind me yelling.

"Run!" he screams with all his strength.

I turn around from curiosity or instinct and see the man being beaten on the floor. I take a step to help him, as he is surrounded by four men. Before I am able to take another step, a horde comes around the corner. They are on the same team as the men attacking the fallen man. One of the four men kills the man on the ground by stabbing him in the back.

Everyone starts to run in my direction, finding a way to scatter. I run. There are too many opponents. Even if I am confident about my fighting skills, I know there are too many of them. They don't run after us. They keep walking. I pass everyone in my way. Even in my weakened state, my body moves faster than everyone else running next to me.

As I make my way, a woman falls beside me. I glance down at her. An arrow has pierced her back. She collapses. I extend my hand. She can only move her eyes. She is paralyzed. Another arrow hits her. She is gone.

I run as the enemy follow. I start to gain distance between them and myself. I make turns from time to time to keep them guessing at the direction I am going. It isn't hard since I have no idea where I am or what any of this used to be.

After running for a while, I can't hear them behind me anymore. I run a bit more, until my body forces me to stop. I fall to the ground. It takes me a second to get

106

VANTABLACK

back on my feet. When I finally do, my stomach pukes, and my vision begins to blur. I fight to stand in place.

A man appears a few feet in front of me. My vision betrays me, and I can't see who it is. The man begins to multiply. I'm still breathing hard, trying to catch my breath. Have they caught up to me? Is this it? I'm about to be put down like a dog. What a way to finish my life.

They walk closer to me. I want to defend myself, but I can hardly stand. One of them grabs me by my clothing, pulls on me, and throws me to the side. I fall to the ground. My heart is beating faster by the second. My vision begins to clear from my left side.

I look at him. He doesn't even bother to look back. I was just an obstacle in his way that needed to be removed. He keeps walking in the direction I came from. The men with him do the same. I now can see only their backs and the weapons they carry. I look past them. The men who were killing people have made their way here. The men in front of me have an elephant either tattooed or on their clothing. They are here to stop the killers.

There is silence. For a second, I hope the other men will leave, but this is not that type of place. No one backs down here. Not long after, they rush one another. Their weapons collide. I hear screams of war and screams of pain. As they fight, I am able to recognize the place: I find myself in the neutral zone, where the markets used to be. I orient myself before taking off. I feel horrible about leaving and not helping them, but I know there is no way for me to help; I would just be another body thrown into the carnage.

I make my way toward the Wolf pack zone. I need to reach them. Finding Miles, Gilligan, and Marcus is my

ZETA

priority. I need answers, and I know they can deliver. If I can find my footing, I can act and do something about the situation. Most importantly, I must find Shanti and be with her. After that, I will find Julius and carve his heart out—that is, if he is still alive in this shattered hell. I know he is still out there; someone so sinister doesn't die that easily.

I try going the way I know, but it is hard to find a path that doesn't have boiling rocks or debris from damaged buildings. I am lucky enough not to run into any more psychopaths with weapons trying to eliminate people.

I finally find the Wolf building. I can't believe my eyes: there is nothing but fire, and parts of the building are covered in debris and collapsing. I fall to my knees. I hoped they were fine and someday would come find me on the lower levels. Now I know that if I hadn't come out, I would have waited for nothing. I realize that whatever happened affected everyone in the bunker. I hold my tears back as my heart fills with sadness and regret for leaving everyone behind as I ran away. I could have stayed with them. I sit there on my knees, trying to gather my thoughts, wondering what happened. What steps led to this disastrous outcome?

As I sit here, I hear someone approaching me. I don't turn to see who it is. I keep looking at the building's flames, which die slowly.

"Let's go."

I recognize the voice. It is Marcus. I look up. He is wearing a dirty cloak, concealing himself. An unstoppable tear escapes from my eye. I get up and ask him what happened here. He doesn't give me an answer. Instead, he asks me to follow him. I assume this

VANTABLACK

isn't a safe place to have a conversation, and we leave at a fast pace. I don't pay much attention to where we are going; I only follow him, as I get caught in my thoughts as the unanswered questions in my head multiply.

We make it to a building I don't recognize. We walk inside. Behind the door are three men guarding with weapons. As I follow Marcus, I glance at the rooms on the way. Most of them have injured people in them, and most of them are civilians. I recognize members of the Wolf pack running around the place. They don't have time to talk; they are too busy gathering food and supplies for the injured. We make our way to the fifth floor. It seems empty, but the people in the rooms on this floor are sleeping. They must have been running around the bunker during the last day and night. Marcus shows me to a room, where he tells me to clean myself and gives me clothes that don't stink of chemicals and filth.

I do as he says. I clean myself as he goes on his way. As I remove the layers of filth covering my skin, I freeze. I can't move. I begin to break like a kid trying to save his sandcastle from collapsing as he cries. Tears run out of my eyes. I don't try to stop them, as I know it is useless. I break in silence; I don't want to alarm anyone. I take a moment to allow myself to feel again, and just like that, I shut the doors. I collect myself and finish what I am doing.

I walk out of the room, looking for Marcus, but he is nowhere to be found. I walk to the fourth floor, but I only find people cleaning weapons and gear on half the floor and stacking medicine and medical supplies on the other. Afterward, I look around the third floor, which only has food being rationed, and then the second floor.

ZETA

I look, but most of the doors are closed or have people crying behind them. As I am about to exit the second floor, I hear a voice I recognize behind one of the doors. The view is limited, but I can see inside the room. It is Eleonore; she is reading to some kids. It seems they are getting ready to go to sleep. She is facing them, so I see only her back as she holds the book in her hands. I stand quietly at the door and listen.

"Now, this is the law of the jungle, as old and as true as the sky," she says without missing a beat.

I stay there listening without bothering them. Word by word, I try to remember what she says. I have never read this book, but the words find a place close to my heart. The kids listen without making a sound. They are amazed by the story. Eventually, she finishes the story. I take another glance at the room. Eleonore turns to the side. I am able to see the book. It has scratches on the cover and looks as if it has been burned a little. Then I notice the inside of it. It is filled with burned and torn pages. She has read them the whole story by memory, I suppose.

A hand grabs my shoulder from behind. I turn. It's Marcus. He has made food for me. We walk back to the fifth floor, where we sit. Gilligan is there waiting for us. I place my food on the table and hug him, and then we sit down. I ask them what has happened. Marcus tells me to eat, and then we can talk. Gilligan brings me a glass of lemonade, and they both patiently watch me eat, exchanging glances from time to time.

I can feel the tension growing. They have something important to tell me. I finish my plate and drink the lemonade in one go. Gilligan serves me some more with a smile. Gilligan sits down, and Marcus has his hands

VANTABLACK

on the table as he stands. They are having a hard time telling me whatever is on their minds.

"Is everything all right?" I ask.

"A lot has happened since you left. Things have changed for everyone for the worse," Marcus says as he rubs the back of his neck.

"Well, what's going on? Why don't you guys catch me up to speed, or are we waiting for Miles to get this started?" I try to get rid of the uncomfortable pauses that keep happening. The silence augments the tension in the room.

"Well, it's hard to—" Gilligan is having a hard time finding the words he wants to say. He stops to find the right way to elaborate on the events that have occurred in my absence.

Marcus says, "The morning we went for you, one of our friends in the Elephant pack delivered us a message. He pounded on the door until someone opened. One of the doorman that night called Miles. He delivered the message."

I have a feeling all this is connected to me in some way.

"The message was that you had killed Julius's girlfriend and stolen her necklace. In order to avoid a war, the Tiger pack was going to let the Elephants deal with it and bring you to justice. Miles called for us immediately. We all met near your place, and that's when we had you run away and hide."

I am still trying to figure out why they are having so much trouble starting this conversation.

"After you left, we took Shanti to her brother and made our way back to the Wolf building. We knew they would come knocking sooner rather than later. When

111

ZETA

the colonel from the Elephants came to the door, Miles answered. He was waiting for them by the door the whole time. They asked to come in, and Miles allowed it if they didn't wake the ones who were sleeping. Only the colonel came into the building. The colonel explained the situation and told Miles he needed to turn you in. Miles replied he hadn't seen you that day, since it was too early, and he wouldn't turn you in even if he knew where you were. Miles tried to convince the colonel it was impossible for you to have done what they were accusing you of, telling him you would never kill anyone who wasn't threatening your life or the lives of the people you care about. The colonel replied that several people had watched Shanti walk down the market street while showing off the necklace that once had been around the victim's neck. Miles told the colonel he wouldn't betray you. The colonel explained that he was only asking him to step aside to get to the truth. He said the Tiger pack was demanding blood for blood.

"Miles immediately answered that he wasn't going to step aside. The colonel informed Miles in good faith that if the Elephants couldn't find you, they wanted to search every territory and level of the bunker. Miles told him they were more than welcome to come conduct a onetime search to keep the peace between packs, but if they didn't find anything, they couldn't ask for another one. The colonel agreed to deliver the message to Julius after he searched the bunker himself first. The colonel knew if the Tiger pack found you first, they would take you to Julius and torture you without anybody ever knowing you had been captured."

I know Julius isn't one to boast about what he has done. He will only discuss things that have happened

VANTABLACK

and not things that are happening. The only way anyone would have known I was dead would have been if Julius decided it was time for them to know.

"The Elephants spent the entire day searching for you. They went to your place and then made their way to one territory after another. Level after level. At the end of the day, since they couldn't find you, they had to report to Julius. Julius sent out an announcement to each pack building to let them know he would be conducting a search in every area. He said that in order to maintain good faith among packs, they should allow it. That way, peace and balance would be kept. He said that whoever refused had something to hide, and as such, it would be an offense to him and the justice he was searching for. He told those who agreed to his request to send a member of their pack to deliver the message by the next day, and he would arrange to search the territory. Miles agreed, and so did everyone else, except the Fox pack." Marcus pauses for a second.

I am surprised and intrigued that they would refuse Julius's request.

"Since Julius hadn't heard from them by the next day, he sent someone from his pack for an answer. The leader of the Fox pack told Julius that he owed him nothing and that his business was his alone. He said Julius could take this answer however he wanted. Julius didn't reply to his message."

I don't think much of the answer the Fox pack gave him. Their leader is a charismatic man from what I have heard, but he is not moved by threats or attempts to intimidate him, even though the Tiger pack is larger than the Fox pack, and their territories are right next to each other.

113

ZETA

"As he had declared, Julius made his way to each territory one by one. Each pack allowed him into their headquarters to search for you. He did one territory per day. He didn't bother going to the Fox pack's building. He left the Wolves for last. Miles accompanied him as his men looked all over for any hiding place or clues to where you might have hidden. Miles told me something that day after they left. He told me Julius didn't seem eager to find you. Julius didn't even say anything to him as his men searched, which was odd. Julius enjoys a monologue during serious times. It has always been part of his damned insanity. We didn't think much of it.

"For the next couple of days, Julius's men searched on each level, from the very top to the very bottom of the bunker. Since they couldn't find you, Julius ordered his men to go back to his base. We all thought it was over. It didn't take him even a day after not being able to find you to make his move."

I hear Marcus's voice change slightly, as if it wants to break as he tries to speak. He and Gilligan look up for a second. Before I can turn, Eleonore passes from behind me to join us in the conversation. She leans against the wall and gives me a smile that seems forced for some reason. Marcus continues where he left off.

"It was already lights-out, and the streets were empty. Silence ruled all around the bunker. I can't remember ever hearing silence in here, but that night, I did. Gilligan and I were back at our place, sleeping, when it happened. Explosions came from every direction. After the detonations, everything was so quiet I could hear only the fires crackle. Not even a minute later, the screams of women and children took over. The headquarters of the packs Julius had searched had

114

VANTABLACK

exploded, except for the Snake pack. We ran toward the Wolf building. Miles was helping some of the injured out of the building, which was covered in flames. We could see him from a distance. Before we could get near him, we noticed many groups of Tigers and Snakes surrounding the front of the building. Julius and Kristov were on the front lines. There was nothing we could do. Miles saw us running toward him. When our eyes met, he shook his head, telling us not to get near. He held Eleonore before giving us one of the signals we use."

Marcus makes a sign with his hand. The moment I see it, I know what it means. When I arrived, I had to memorize a lot of signs used as code for Wolves. That sign signaled to all the other Wolves, "Save the rest, and leave me to die." I turn to Eleonore, and she holds a hand over her mouth, trying to keep herself from breaking down as she cries.

"I'm sorry." That is all I can say as a tear runs down my face as I look at her. She takes a deep breath, trying to regain her composure. I don't know what to say. *What do you say to a person whose world was taken from her because of you?* I turn my head, looking down at the table, as I hold my hands together.

"Don't—" She still is trying to gather herself enough to speak. She feels the need to say what she has to say. "Don't you dare."

I am speechless.

"Every day you spent together, he told me you were different. He saw part of himself in you—a fire that this bunker suffocated until it was extinguished. He told me he believed in you and said you could change things around you if you were just given the chance. He saw something in you. So you don't get to be sorry."

ZETA

Tears run down my face nonstop.

"When we were outside as the building burned behind us, he held me. He kissed me and whispered in my ear that none of this was your fault. Even as death was at his door, he took the time to explain to me what it took me a while to understand. This was meant to happen, whether it was you to blame or someone else. But Julius made the mistake to blame you for it and not kill you. Now you are here. Miles believed in you and the change you could bring around you, and we need that now more than we ever will. I believe in you, because he showed me what he saw in you that made him believe."

I never knew Miles felt that way about me, an orphan. Her words make me want to believe in the fire Miles saw in me. I just hope that what I went through while I was absent hasn't changed me inside so much that the past me is completely gone.

"As Miles gave the signal, some of the other injured Wolves did the same. They wanted to allow the rest to escape. We knew he didn't want us to stay and fight. He was telling us to protect the rest and help them escape as they gave us an opening."

I turn to look at Marcus as he explains how everything happened.

"Miles and the rest of the injured Wolves formed a barrier, protecting the others. They fought as the rest ran for safety. Miles took Julius and Kristov on. We ran to help the rest get out of the wall the Tigers and Snakes had formed. They weren't letting anyone escape. We hit them from behind, and they broke formation. Gilligan ran to grab Eleonore, and we all made our escape, leaving the rest behind. We saw the fight from a distance as we ran."

VANTABLACK

He takes a moment and then continues. "Miles kept fighting to the very end. Fierce. They couldn't take him down. Finally, they all charged and outmanned them. Miles kept swinging until Kristov stabbed him in the back. Julius took the front and cut Miles. They became enraged as they cut him. They knew from his smile that they could kill him, but they could never break him. Julius stabbed him on one side, and Kristov stabbed him on the other, killing him. He died there, and as we ran, the flames grew wilder. The fire illuminated Miles's face, revealing his defiant smile, which he kept until the very end."

Till it's lights-out, I say in my head, picturing Miles.

I need to fix this. I have been a piece in the game Julius orchestrated. The tears that run down my face remind me that I can still feel. Maybe I didn't change as much as I thought when I was down there. Either way, I feel something inside me trying to break out. This thing Julius has started is fueling something in me. I want to run into the streets and yell his name until he shows his face. I know it isn't the time to act on impulse. I just sit here, waiting for them to finish filling the gaps of the events that have led us to this point in time.

Gilligan takes over to finish explaining. "After that, it was clear the Tiger and Snake packs were allies. They started hunting the injured, taking their weapons, food, and anything they wanted. They made their way to the Fox headquarters that same night. They had Molotovs ready to burn the whole building down. They yelled the Fox leader's name, telling him to come out and surrender. Tobaqui came out, and they threatened to kill anyone who followed him. He walked down the steps of the building alone. He ordered everyone else to

117

ZETA

stay inside. They say he had to knock Zack out, because Zack wouldn't allow him to go alone. He was ready to die with Tobaqui, but Tobaqui wouldn't allow it. Julius and Kristov knew Tobaqui was too strong for them to take on, especially now that Miles had injured them."

As Gilligan continues to talk, I fight myself. I want to act, but all I can do is wait.

"They ordered their men to get him, but Tobaqui wasn't going down that easy. He took them on, breaking bones and injuring them as they rushed him in wave after wave. He fought valiantly. Everyone knew his strength was incomparable, but they were too many. In the end, they subdued him. They had him on his knees, and his face was covered in blood. That was when those cowards moved in to finish the job. After they took him out, they stepped into the building. In the entrance, Zack was lying down on the floor, regaining consciousness. He could see Tobaqui's dead body lying on the street. He lost control and wanted to kill them both right then. He was able to get up and take a shot at Kristov. Shanti was in the room, screaming for it all to stop."

I fear the worst is to come. My heart starts beating faster. I can feel myself losing control, and whatever has awakened in me is clawing its way out.

"Julius told Kristov to leave it alone, but he refused. He demanded payback. He kicked Zack down onto the ground and called one of his men for a sword. He swung down, cutting the arm Zack had used to strike him. The sword was a fire type we had delivered. It cut his arm, and there was no bleeding. Zack screamed. Kristov wanted to cut the other one too, but Julius walked in front of Kristov as he held the blade. He ordered Zack

VANTABLACK

to sit up straight. Julius told him he was now the leader of the Fox pack. He told him to do a better job than Tobaqui had done in following orders, or next time, he would be the one lying out there. Shanti ran over and held Zack close. After that, they left the building and went on their way."

For a second, I feel glad. I was worried Gilligan was going to tell me Kristov had cut down Shanti. I feel the rage simmer inside me.

No one says anything after that. That is all that has happened since I left. It is a lot to take in at once. We have to formulate a plan—anything to stop the chaos that has been brought down upon us. I'm not the only one who is dealing with something. Eleonore, Gilligan, and Marcus are all trying to cope with it too. The time for action hasn't arrived yet; we need to formulate a plan to come back from the ashes we have been burned down to. We stay here in silence. The fact that they haven't made a move against the Tigers and Snakes yet means one of two things: they don't have a plan yet, or they are still trying to stand back up after the devastating blow they have taken.

I question them about their plan to take the battle to Julius and Kristov. As I suspect, they are still attempting to get back on their feet. Most of the Wolves who made it out are busy trying to gather weapons and food after finding shelter in this place. They have no news from the other packs yet, only small details of the day when everyone was attacked.

The Elephants have suffered losses too, but since they weren't located in one single place during the attack, they still have plenty of manpower to take a stand. However, they have to fight the Snake and Tiger

ZETA

pack members who are scattered around the bunker and wreaking havoc, and it is hard for them to protect everyone when there are more enemies. It is going to be a hard battle.

"Do you think the other packs will join us when we go against the Tigers and Snakes?" I ask, looking at them. I get up from my seat and start to pace. They look at each other.

"Packs don't follow one another. They may go as far as to call a truce, but they won't let anybody else call the shots for their people," Gilligan answers.

"They are scared their packs will think, *What kind of leader follows someone else?*" Marcus adds.

I have no response. I have to find a way to get them to unite. If we all join to attack the Tigers and Snakes, we will be able to end this and maybe even get their men to surrender when they see they are outnumbered. Time is of the essence. If we wait for more days to pass, we might fail. The other packs might end up being hunted down or too weak to fight. There is a lot to do in little time.

"Tomorrow we will visit them and try to persuade them to help end this. We only have to convince the two packs left: the Apes and the Foxes." I believe this is the way to go.

"They won't follow anybody," Gilligan says.

"We have to try. If we don't, we might as well just wait to die here. The longer we wait, the weaker we become. Who knows what they are doing out there running free? They might be planning how to take us out as we speak," I say, not letting my frustration get the best of me. "If we get them to fight with us, we have a chance at stopping this. The Elephants are already

120

VANTABLACK

fighting, but they can't do it alone. We can't just sit around surviving, waiting for someone else to save us. There's no one coming for us in our darkest moment. It's up to us and only us."

Eleonore nods. Marcus looks around and then agrees. Gilligan is on board. He doesn't want to argue the same point once everyone is on the same page.

"Be ready before the lights are on. We will have to cover a lot of ground, and most of it will be in searching for them. If we can at least get one pack to side with us, we might be able to give them a proper fight. We will speak with the Elephant pack after we have gathered enough men to fight. There's no need to convince them, since they are already taking the fight to them whether we help or don't. We might be able to get a cease-fire with them if we don't get them to follow us," I say.

They agree. Eleonore leaves the room first. After that, we all go rest. We have an arduous day ahead of us. We will rest until the moment comes to give it our best in carrying out the plan.

I lie in bed that night unable to sleep. I keep rolling and twisting without any luck. Thought after thought keeps me awake. It is impossible to find something else to focus on. My thoughts keep going from what happened in the bunker to Miles's no longer being here. Then I think about Shanti, wondering how she is handling all this. How am I going to convince the Ape or Fox pack to follow us? My brain is restless. Hour after hour passes without even a minute of sleep.

My mind tortures me with fictional scenarios and memories of what I have lived through—the time I have spent in the Wolf pack and the time I have spent in the darkness. I don't feel like myself anymore, or

Z E T A

maybe this is who I have always been. Something dark and macabre has been planted in me, or maybe it has always been there and now has been awakened. I think of what led me to deserve all of this. Maybe I haven't been a good person, with all the suffering I have brought onto others by collecting debts or walking away from those who were hungry before I met Shanti. I convinced myself I was a good person while I was with her, but now that she isn't with me, I have different thoughts. *What if I have always been a bad person trying to act like a good one?* I can't remember doing anything that can be considered good without Shanti by my side. I am like a demon who steals some wings to trick the angels into thinking he is one of them to enjoy heaven. What if all this suffering is something I deserve, and I have brought it to everyone else trapped in this cage with me? Maybe this is hell, and the facade has finally stopped. The world's nature finally has struck the flimsy tower of our reality, unveiling how the world really is. It has all come down to sinking or swimming as the sharks surround us, waiting to end us when they feel it is time.

I don't like that my thoughts become more negative as the night keeps dragging. There isn't anything to do about it, however, so I welcome the way changes are happening inside my head.

Eleven

The next morning comes after a long night without sleep. I don't feel tired. I walk with purpose as I head down the stairs of the building. Marcus and Gilligan are already there, covering themselves and their weapons under cloaks. Gilligan hands me my cloak with one hand and a sword with the other. Eleonore comes down the stairs with an apple for each of us. She wants to come help, but she has a duty with the kids who need care. She is no stranger to fighting. Miles once told me they met a long time ago when she would constantly fight. Seeing her drives my thoughts toward Miles and the fact that he is gone. What I wouldn't give for one more conversation with him as we walk down the street. I always wanted to ask him about his upbringing. He always talked about the past with a smile, even the painful moments. Eleonore, Gilligan, and Marcus were always in the memories he shared with me.

I take the apple and thank her. She gives me a smile. We walk out of the building into the havoc Julius has created in the bunker. The fires burning some of the buildings have died down. The smoke is still present, but it seems to be clearing out. We follow Gilligan, as he is the one who knows where the Apes are gathered. After walking for a while, we see some of the Snake

ZETA

pack members running around searching for their next prey. They are in groups. It is hard to tell how many there are sometimes.

We keep our eyes open for danger and hide ourselves from the enemy. We don't know how far away from each other each group of the Snake pack is. That makes it hard to fight them without running into an ambush. We run into a large group of the Elephant militia. They don't bother us. They are searching for the Snakes. If they don't see an emblem of a snake on our clothing, it doesn't matter what we are doing. They can tell we are hiding and trying to get from one place to another without running into those savages.

They are a proud group, the Elephants. They don't hide themselves, and they walk from one place to another, hoping to run into the enemy. They believe in their calling. They want to end this and restore order. They keep walking past us.

We keep going for a few more miles before running into trouble. We can hear a small group of Snakes just around the corner where Gilligan has stopped us. He peeks with caution. There are five of them standing in the middle of the street. We have to cross over without them seeing us, but there is too much space from one end of the street to the other. They will see us without any problem. Gilligan gives Marcus a signal. Marcus tells me to draw my sword as he whispers. There is no other way. We either charge them now or wait for them to catch up to us as we cross the street and fight them then. We get ready.

I don't feel nervous. We have been doing this since before all this happened. Maybe I have grown desensitized. I've fought so many times while working

124

VANTABLACK

for the Wolves that this doesn't feel any different. My adrenaline starts pumping. My body is getting ready for a fight.

Gilligan runs first, and Marcus follows. I take a deep breath and follow. We run with both hands on our swords. One of the Snakes notices us running toward them. He tries to alert those around him. By that time, we are already at a deadly distance. Gilligan takes the right side, cutting one of them from behind on the back of the neck. At the same time, Marcus takes the guy who spotted us, driving his sword through his chest. Their eyes are on Marcus. They shake as they try to pull out their knives and hammers. They try to swing at him, but I am here. I take one of them out with a swing. Gilligan is already taking out another. When I turn around to get the remaining one, Marcus has already cut him down.

They never stood a chance. Marcus and Gilligan have seen violence from the start, just as Miles did. They grew up during one of the many wars that happened in the bunker before I was even born. Most of the Snake pack are psychopaths but have no idea how taking enemies works. From what we have seen, they enjoy hurting others and play with their victims, taking their time. Once you find yourself in a battle, you keep going until it's over. If you swing your sword once, you don't stop. You pause only to change direction for your next swing. There's a lot of stamina involved. I am glad I have walked up the stairs outside the wall so many times. I don't break a sweat.

We put our swords away and look around us. The area is clear. Gilligan continues to run, and we follow.

We finally make it to our destination. The building looks severely damaged. There is no one protecting the

ZETA

front entrance. I am skeptical, but this is supposedly the place the Apes are using as shelter. We try to open the door, but it doesn't move much; it is stopped by something on the other side. We see someone peeking out. The man recognizes Gilligan, who has been friends with some of the members of this pack in the past. The man opens the door. After we walk inside, the Apes place a heavy piece of furniture to block the entrance again.

The man who opened the door leads us to their leader. I look around as we make our way to him. The people in this place aren't doing much better than we are. They seem to be barely hanging on. They seem weak. Some of them are not able to stand up, so they sit on the floor as they guard the perimeter.

We finally make it to the room where the leader of the Apes is. He is finishing a conversation with one of his followers. Everyone leaves the room as we walk in. The man leading us signals for us to stop. He approaches the leader and whispers in his ear. He looks back at us and then tells us to approach his leader. He proceeds to leave the room, closing the door behind him.

"Gilligan, old friend, what brings you to my side of hell this morning?" the man says as he walks around a desk, holding on to it in his weakened state.

"We are here to ask for your help against the ones who made this cursed bunker worse," Gilligan answers with a smile. "These are my friends. They asked me to bring them here to join forces and help us all reclaim our lives. We believe we have a better chance of ending this quickly if we all work together, King."

"Is that so?" King pauses for a second as he tries to sit on his chair. "Why would my men follow someone

VANTABLACK

else who is not their leader? Is this the disrespect you come in today with, Gilligan? You come to ask me to give away my position as leader of my people just like that, as if it is nothing? Huh?"

Gilligan apologizes and tries to explain to King, but he has no intention of listening. He raises a hand and points us to the door.

I interrupt. "No one is asking you to give anything up. We have come to make a deal. You help us, and we help you. At the end of all of this, we'll go back to the way things were and call all of this a bad dream."

Gilligan turns to look at me and then at King.

King is staring at me, and his frown turns into a sarcastic smile. "Well, what is it you have in mind for us to do, young one?" he asks as he sits up straight in his chair.

"I can see you have a lot of men out there. They all seem like they have been in a fight before. Why don't you help us lead a charge against the Tigers and Snakes? We'll attack both of them at once and end everything in one day. Put them all down so there's no retaliation after, and then we can all go back to regaining what was taken from us," I say. My plan isn't much of a plan.

"How do you think they will see me if I let someone else take over my leadership? Who is going to follow a man whose hand can be twisted to let go of his command so easily? You might have lived in this bunker and joined a pack, but you still have much to learn. We don't call each other animal names just because of how it sounds. We are all animals, plain and simple. We call each other humans to make ourselves feel superior to a monkey, a wolf, or even a snake, but the truth is, when it comes down to it, our instincts take over, and

ZETA

we are just the same. Where have you been? Have you seen what's happening out there? People fighting each other over whatever food and water they find. They are fighting each other so much that by the time the Snakes come, they are already too weak to fight them too. You come here and make requests as if things are as simple as passing bread at the table. We are hungry, kid. All we have right now are those we are loyal to and the food we can get our hands on to eat. If the food stops flowing, so does the loyalty soon after. My men are out there searching for food day in and day out. When they find some, they bring it back and give it to some of them to eat, and the rest watch them. The next day, the ones who already ate go out and gather what they can to feed the next ones. They eat one day, and they wait a day. One day they will come back without any food, or they will grow tired of this system and never come back. Then the pack will be gone, and whoever doesn't get killed by the Snakes will live in Julius's bunker until they die, or they'll join him. I won't give up on my men and let someone else make the calls. I will lead them until they say they have had enough and leave me to rot. What do you know about leadership, kid? You have never led anything in your life. It's a different world when you are the one wearing the crown, and you walk in here to ask me to give you mine? You must be out of your mind."

He is right. I know nothing about leading a pack and having to remain unbreakable in the eyes of those who follow.

"I don't give a damn about your crown!" I say. I have to persuade him somehow. "Your men are out there dying, and you are so insecure you can't see past

VANTABLACK

what they will think of you if you form an alliance? What kind of leader are you? Leaders are out there with their men, putting in the work. They lead by example and inspire their men. They'd rather go down to make sure their people have a chance to make it than protect their imaginary crown. You would rather they betray you than save them by following someone else's plan? I'm not asking you to give up what you have worked so hard to keep. I'm asking you to be part of a plan to give the people you care about a chance to get out of the suffering that's surrounding them. A leader is supposed to be the light for his people, even when the fire burns him as he holds it up high for them to see. Stand with us. Be part of the plan. We are not asking you to follow us. We are asking you to lend a hand to another pack in a fight. We'll both fight them our way and reclaim our place in this bunker we are forced to stay in. What good is a leader if his followers are dying out there one by one as he beats his head while trying to think of a way to change things? As far as everyone is concerned, we are here to ask you to cut a deal: we'll pay you with food and water for your people, and you'll agree to fight by our side. That's all it is. Just another deal between packs."

He stares at me. His sarcastic smile is gone. He stands up slowly from his chair in the weakened body that governs him. He walks up to me and looks at me from head to toe before giving me an answer.

"And if we don't help you, then what? You will not bring the food? Or what if I agree with you, and after we have eaten, I change my mind now that I can think clearly with a full stomach? What's your plan then, young'un?" He turns to look at Gilligan and Marcus and then returns his gaze to me.

ZETA

"Then you and your people will be in good shape to fight whoever comes after you if we don't succeed," I say.

He backs away in confusion at my answer.

"But if we do finish this, no one will ever forget the time the leader of the Apes decided to hide as other men freed him. You can stay here, but I doubt the Elephants will let you live the day they saved you go unnoticed to the people." I say what I have to say, and Marcus, Gilligan, and I turn around and walk toward the door. We have to talk to the Fox pack and the Elephant pack, and we can't waste the entire day with one pack who doesn't want to help.

"The Elephant militia is still fighting out there?" King asks.

"Where have you been? Haven't you seen what's happening out there?" Marcus answers.

I say, "We will have our men get food and have it delivered to you here. You can join us or not. We still have two more hardheaded leaders to talk into joining forces. I can't spend the whole day with you. We have a bunker to stop from burning down."

King stares at us as we walk away. It is up to him after that.

We make our way out of the building and walk toward the Fox zone. I order Gilligan to head back to base and have some of our men go collect food. He is to have them fed, rested, and ready for when they have to go out. He goes on his way as Marcus and I keep running toward our destination. After making it to the Fox zone, we stop, seeing Snakes patrolling the streets. It seems they are steering clear of the Fox zone, so we don't have to keep fighting. We walk the rest of the

130

VANTABLACK

way, still cautious in case it's a trap to make us let our guard down.

We finally make it to the Fox base. There are two men outside, guarding the door. We approach them with our bodies and faces still covered. We ask to speak to their leader, and they ask us to remove our cloaks, which conceal our identities. Marcus takes off his. As soon as they see him, they don't wait for me to remove mine. They launch at us, trying to capture us. We don't use our weapons, not wanting to injure them, and they don't draw theirs. We start fighting, making noise in the street. After a while, another member of their pack opens the door, telling us to stop. Zack sees us from the top floor and commands his men to stand down, allowing us to have a word with him for now.

When we enter the building, his men are armed, and they seem ready for battle. The man who stopped the fight outside leads us toward the back. As we enter the room in the back, Zack is walking down the stairs. His arm is gone, and he has a dead stare in his eyes, as if his spirit has been broken. He makes his way toward Marcus and me.

"You shouldn't be here. The Snake pack is searching for you, and I can't afford to be seen with anyone who isn't allied to them." Zack walks past us to the entrance of the room.

He doesn't even look us in the eye as he talks to us. What happened that day broke him heavily. He doesn't seem like the man I met before. It's like talking to a ghost of the man I met before.

"Are you saying we are your enemies too?" Marcus asks calmly.

Zack can't give us an answer. He only asks us to

ZETA

state our business so we can be on our way. I can't believe it, but I have to. He doesn't have to say it; I know he is on the side of Julius and Kristov. They must have done a number on him to break him down, take part of him away, and still have him be on their side.

I say, "We are leading an attack against them soon. We want you to be part of it and avenge—"

He doesn't let me finish my sentence. "I'm with them now!" He raises his voice. It is the first time he has shown emotion. "I swore I was going to avenge Tobaqui, and I couldn't. They took my arm, and they threatened to take Shanti too if I didn't follow their orders. They want me to have my men ready to move into every level to gather the survivors of their attack. Anybody caught with a pack is as good as dead. I already lost someone I cared for; I can't lose another one. I will kill you both before I let something happen to her."

I can feel his pain in every word. I want to ask about Shanti, but I know this isn't the time. I have to get him to calm down.

"Fight with us. I promised you I would keep Shanti safe, and I will, but now I need your help to keep everyone else safe too. We can change it all; we just need to work together. I won't let anything happen to her. I just need you to stop being afraid of them and stand back up to fight by our side," I say.

"Safe? Who are you going to save? You left as all the pieces came crumbling down. You took some time off as we tried to protect what mattered to us as it was cut down. I'm not afraid of them or what they are doing out there. I just can't let them come back here to take everything else I have left. They are too strong, and

VANTABLACK

you are just being hopeful in thinking you can change anything at all."

"We can. No one is saying it will be easy, but if we work together, we can make a difference. We can reclaim our lives. If you don't, then for the rest of your days, until they decide, your life won't be yours. All you must do is not give up. Unite your strength with ours, and let's make them pay."

"I can't," he answers.

"Yes, you can."

"You don't understand," he replies.

"Help me understand."

"I gave up!" he yells. Silence takes over the room. "I saw the madness and the anger they held inside them. All this time, they were holding it inside because they knew they couldn't be that way. All the evil things they held all these years kept growing, and now that they are the ones calling the shots, they have no reason to hide it. They are letting everyone else see the way the world is inside their heads. We are living in their insanity. How do you plan to fight their madness?" He looks into my eyes, and tears want to escape his eyes. He turns away to hide his pain.

It is the first time he has looked directly at me this whole time. They didn't just kill Tobaqui and cut his arm off; they also threatened the thing he cares about most in his life. His hands are tied, and he is drowning, with nowhere to go. They left him without options. The only thing he can do is fall in line. Going against them isn't an option if it means losing Shanti. I understand his position.

"I don't know," I say, and he turns to look at me. "All I know is that we have to fight back. For ourselves

133

ZETA

and for everyone else who can't stand for himself. If we don't, we are part of the problem for standing by. I will keep going at them until I go down or they do. The more of us there are, the better chance we have at winning. I don't mind going down if it means someone else gets to live. Having Shanti and your men live trapped and at the mercy of insane men is not living. If they are insane, who knows when they will come banging on the door to take what they want? If you can't stop them now, how will you stop them then? When Kristov decides he wants to take Shanti with him, how will you stop him? You promised me you would take care of her, and I told you I would do the same. So if I die after attacking them, I just hope you can keep her safe. You might have given up, but the battle is still happening out there, and if you do what they ask, you will only be helping them finish everything easier. I really hope you are as strong as Tobaqui when they come for you, and you don't regret the decision you have made here. Keep Shanti safe for me if I don't come back." I finish saying what I have to say.

Silence takes over as I wait for him to say something. After a while, I hear steps coming down the stairs. It is Shanti. When her eyes lock with mine, I walk to the bottom of the stairs and wait for her. She rushes into my arms and holds me as hard as she can. I grab her hand and kiss it, immensely happy to see her again. She caresses my face with her other hand. I have no words to say. I forget about the world for a moment as I hold her close to me. It's just the two of us.

"He doesn't just want me to gather all the survivors from each level and bring them here. He also wants me to hand them over to the Snake pack. I don't know what

VANTABLACK

they plan to do with them, but I can imagine. I know where Julius and Kristov are. If we were to help you, can you end them? Can you bring them down and stop their madness from eradicating us all?" Zack asks as he looks down at the floor.

I turn to him and give him a nod. Either he believes in me, or he wants to give everyone a chance, especially Shanti. Maybe seeing her has changed his mind and reminded him of what he needs to do to protect her.

"I'll have my men ready for battle," Zack tells me.

We have to go, but I am dying to stay. I haven't seen Shanti since the day I left. I take a step away, and she grips my hand firmly. She also wants me to stay. I look into her eyes as they invite me to take a moment for ourselves. I have to fight the part of me that wants to take a moment to be with her. I know our time is limited outside. No one knows how much time we have, only Julius and Kristov. We have to hurry our plan before they are ready to finish theirs. I hold her close and kiss her. She lets go of my hand. I pull myself away and give her a smile. She is surprised and playfully mad at me for doing so. She smiles from ear to ear.

"I will be all yours as soon as I put an end to this," I say as I walk backward, looking at my beloved Shanti.

"Promise?" she asks as she watches me leave.

I answer her with a smile. I am going to make it up to her for this nightmare.

We leave the Fox building and start walking. I notice Marcus keeps looking at me, so I question him about it. He laughs before answering.

"You can't stop smiling since you saw her."

I can never tell if I am smiling or not. It is something that keeps happening. She makes me smile. Somehow,

135

ZETA

I feel as if things are not as bad when I am around her. This time is no different. For a second, I forgot about everything happening around us.

We make our way into the streets, looking for the Elephant militia. It takes us a little longer than we expect, but we find them. Luckily, we find them before a large group of the Snakes find us. The Elephant militia are fighting in several areas of the bunker, not just on this level. Marcus has heard that some of the men and women from the bunker have joined to help fight back against Julius and Kristov's men—regular people tired of waiting for death to come knocking at their door. You can only kick people for so long before they stop caring about the pain and start fighting for what they believe is right.

Many people have been affected. I don't want to think of how many kids have been made orphans amid all this chaos. These are dark times in the bunker. From what I have heard, there have been plenty of dark times in this place. I guess it doesn't matter what is around us; we just keep finding a reason to fight one another throughout the ages. This is the first time this has happened since I was born. I don't remember something this cruel ever happening, but then again, I haven't been alive for that long. I want to ask Marcus and Gilligan about how things were before I was born, but I have never found the chance. They aren't much older than I am—maybe a decade or two—but this bunker has seen more than its fair share of blood spilled. It is clear we are far from having peace rule over our lives.

The men from the Elephant militia take us to the colonel once they find out who we are, and we explain why we need to talk to him. It takes some convincing,

VANTABLACK

but Marcus is known from around the bunker. His reputation and his past grant us guidance to see the colonel.

After making several different stops, going through different buildings, and exiting through different areas, we finally make it to the place where the colonel is located. They are being cautious. The colonel doesn't stay for more than one day in a building. He continuously keeps moving to avoid being attacked by his enemies as his men work to protect the lives of the innocent. I am sure that if he fell, his men wouldn't know what to do. They are good men and women fighting for their lives and way of life, but they are no tacticians. The colonel is trying to defend a future for everyone but has failed to get someone to take over command if he ever dies. He is trying to teach each of his subordinates how to survive in our present condition.

We walk into a building that is destroyed. There are only two floors, and all the buildings around it have been burned or torn down. The colonel is on the second floor, talking to his men, gathering intel on the whereabouts of the Snakes and Tigers. He always has two people taking notes. One writes information about the Tigers, and the other writes about the Snakes. Everyone is moving around without making much noise. He has a count of the confirmed men of each group and how many they have killed. He is trying to gather as much information on them as possible to take them all on his own. He is way ahead of us on this part. We have a plan, and he has the information we need. If we join forces, we can both benefit and match our common enemy with manpower.

The man guiding us asks us to wait next to the door

ZETA

of the room as he makes his way to the table. He stands there waiting for the colonel to notice him, to inform him that we are here to talk to him. The colonel is talking to everyone at the table. It is obvious he is busy. The man does not try to interrupt; he just stands there staring at the colonel. I think he is hoping the colonel will notice him so he doesn't have to interrupt him. A couple of minutes pass, and the man still has not said anything to him. I take a step to approach the colonel, but Marcus stops me. He must know something I do not, or he does not want to get on the colonel's bad side when we are trying to gain him as an ally. We keep waiting, but the colonel seems as if he is never going to notice the man standing next to the table to introduce us.

The waiting is driving me insane. I turn to look at Marcus, but he doesn't seem to mind. He is looking at the things on the tables near us. I try to control the sense of urgency that keeps resurfacing. Marcus starts grabbing things and holding them close to examine them with his gaze. I ignore him. I just keep staring at the man who is supposed to introduce us as he stares at the colonel as if trying to use his telepathic powers to get his attention.

A loud noise of glass breaking on the floor makes everyone in the room stop in his tracks. There is complete silence. I look around but can't see where the sound has come from. The colonel straightens up and turns to look in our direction. When I realize the whole room is staring at us, I have an idea of what happened. I turn to Marcus. Sure enough, he has dropped one of the items he was looking at. He doesn't seem to notice, or doesn't seem to care, that everyone is looking at us.

VANTABLACK

The colonel steps around the table to get a clear view of us. The man waiting to introduce us finally does.

"C-C-Colonel, these men are here to talk to you about a way to defeat our enemies and end this battle."

The way he says it, I swear he is about to pass out. The colonel ignores him and asks us to state our business.

"Good of you to notice us, Colonel. I thought we were going to have to wait forever for you to give us the time of day," Marcus says as he tosses another item in his hand onto the table.

I can't believe what I am seeing. He is acting like Gilligan. I wanted him here with me because I believed the colonel would take him more seriously than Gilligan. Did he drop the item on the floor on purpose to get the colonel's attention?

"State your plan of action," the colonel says.

"Colonel, if we could talk privately, I think we would feel more comfortable," I say. A private conversation will ensure he won't overreact if our plan isn't to his liking. I don't want him to act out to show off in front of his men. If he does, he won't be reasonable.

He turns his head and gives a nod. Everyone starts emptying the floor. We wait for everyone to leave and wait a little longer in case anyone is still close enough to hear what we have to say. As soon as the area is clear, Marcus and I start explaining our plan.

I begin. "We came here to ask for your help in defeating Julius and Kristov. We have a plan of attack, and it will work a lot better if we have the strength of your men with us. It will greatly reduce the risk of everyone involved. We figure since they are our enemies, well,

ZETA

we don't have to be friends, but at least we can call a cease-fire between us and help each other out."

The colonel's facial expression tells me he is not on board at all. "Why would we join forces with you? From what we have gathered, the Wolf pack is barely holding on, and we are still standing our ground against the Snake pack," he says as he tries to keep a strong front.

"Come on, Donovan. Why are you acting like your men are not barely holding on?" Marcus says nonchalantly. "We have noticed your men out there fighting battle after battle against the Snakes. If I correctly remember, you never had this many men before."

As the colonel adjusts himself, I can see that Marcus is going in the right direction.

"With that being said, either you found a way to grow kids into men very quickly to recruit them, or you are letting civilians join you to be able to fight the Snakes."

The colonel does not bother to correct Marcus, since he is not wrong. Some of the people wearing an elephant emblem seem to have never fought a day in their lives. Most of them are mothers or fathers who have worked nonstop to stay alive. They have no time to be getting into brawls or fighting one another.

"So you gave a bunch of inexperienced people weapons to fight and can't even train them before sending them to get killed? That's coldhearted," I say, adding some commentary to support Marcus.

"Hell, some of their weapons are probably from their homes, from their own kitchens." Marcus pauses for a second and takes a step toward the colonel. "Now you want to look me in the eye, Donovan, and tell me

VANTABLACK

you don't need any help in fighting back? What are some kitchen knives and forks going to do against arrows and swords?"

"I even heard some of them have guns with some extra bullets to waste," I add.

"That's enough!" the colonel shouts. "We are the only ones out there fighting, while everyone else is hiding. You do not get to tell me how I can or can't win battles. We lose some, yes, but we win others. We are the only thing standing against them to stop them from taking over the whole bunker. If they weren't so busy fighting us, all of you would already be dead by their hands. You and everyone else are lying low, trying to stand as the whole ground is shaking below you. These men and women wanted to fight, and I was not about to deny them that right. If we save people and they decide they want to fight back against the Snakes and the Tigers, who are we to say no?"

I can tell we have struck a nerve. I try to come up with something to say to be able to leave with him on our side, but I am drawing a blank.

"No one is telling you what you can or can't do, Donovan. I'm simply stating what I can see from being out there a few minutes a day. Now, if I can notice that, what makes you think they can't?"

The colonel is surprised. He looks at us, but he has nothing to say.

"That's all we wanted to say. You obviously don't need our help in standing your ground and giving them a good fight, holding them off day after day until one goes down." Marcus, seemingly done saying his part, turns to look at me.

"We are going to fight them on our own then. We

ZETA

have gathered enough people to fight back; we just thought we might join forces and finish this quickly." As I talk, I can see the colonel has been doubting the outcome of the fight in the long run. "That's all. We had to ask, but if the answer is no, there's not much we can do."

The colonel seems like he wants to stop us as we turn around and are about to exit the room. I feel something inside tell me that he is not going to reach out for us. His pride is too much to let him ask for help.

"We have some extra weapons hidden in a safe place. We will have some of our men bring you what we can to this place. I'm guessing your people will have a better chance to make it if they have the right weapons," I add as we walk out the door.

The colonel doesn't try to stop us. We walk out of the building without looking back. We hope he will send someone, if he can't do it himself, to tell us we have a truce, but that is just wishful thinking. We make our way back to the building we've been hiding in.

Twelve

When we arrive, Gilligan has taken some of the men to gather food from the lower levels, as I told him to. It seems they are on their way to give the Apes the food they need to recover. Everyone in the building is eating by the time we arrive. I ask those who are still able to move to head back to the place where Marcus and Gilligan's shop was. Marcus tells them where he has some stashed weaponry hidden and how to get it.

I have them count every person who can fight and wants to. After that, they bring enough weapons for everyone here to use. Some of them already have some, but I insist. I have them deliver the rest to the building where the Elephant pack is staying for the night. As they make their way, Marcus and I take some time to eat and come up with a plan of attack.

Eleonore comes and picks up our plates, and she brings us something to drink as we start talking about a way to defeat Julius and Kristov. Marcus and I stand on opposite sides of the table. We have to come up with a plan in case the Elephant pack help us and a second plan in case they don't.

Either way, Marcus says we have to be the ones to take Julius on. We have heard he took all his people to the highest levels of the bunker, leaving Kristov to do

ZETA

as he pleases down here. We can't make the Ape and Fox packs take on the Snakes alone. We know the Apes will think they are being used. King will try to find a way to get out of helping us, even after we helped him. We can't allow him to make an excuse to leave before the fight or halfway through it. We keep debating our course of action.

After a few hours, we are both tired of thinking. I can feel a headache coming. We allow ourselves a minute to rest, to avoid coming up with a faulty plan.

Marcus scratches his head as I massage the back of my neck. I turn to look at him. I have a question on my mind.

"Did you drop that item back at the Elephant pack on purpose?" I ask, trying to avoid laughing.

"No, it slipped from my hands, and I decided to go somewhere with it. I'm just glad it didn't backfire on us. Donovan can be a hard-ass sometimes," he answers.

"I noticed that you called him Donovan a lot. Were you guys close before all of this happened?"

"Something like that. We all knew each other back before we became what we are now. We all grew up together in a way. Donovan, Gilligan, Miles, Kristov, and I were close before the last war of the packs."

I wonder why this is the first time I am hearing about this. He has my full attention. "Kristov?" I say.

"Yeah. Believe it or not, he, Donovan, and Miles grew up together even before Gilligan and I met them. They were inseparable. We all met each other young. We stayed in touch even after we all chose packs to work for when we turned eighteen. Miles and Kristov chose the Wolves. Eventually Kristov left and joined the Snakes. Gilligan and I went a different route. Gilligan

144

VANTABLACK

took the Bear emblem, and I took the Panther. Donovan went his own way."

"Bear? Panther?"

"Before, there were more packs. After people came to the bunker, they started to form groups. Then those groups became packs. There were more than a few packs on every level, from the very top of the bunker all the way to the bottom. It didn't matter how much they tried to have peace; eventually, they would fight each other. One by one, they disappeared. After so many wars among them, people stopped joining them to avoid having to fight every day against others just because they were in another pack. When we were kids, there were only a few packs left. The packs that survived after so many years decided they would all stay on this level and not involve everyone else in what they had going on."

I am amazed at what I am hearing. I have never heard the history of the packs that are still around to this day. Maybe I never bothered to pay attention.

"Even when we were part of different packs, we still made time to see each other from time to time. Slowly, we stopped. Everyone had his own life. Until one day, another war began. Some packs wanted more territory and more food. That was what most wars were about— wanting more and more and never being content with what they had. Two packs decided to join and start reducing the number of the other ones. Slowly, without telling anyone, they become allies. Not long after, the other packs noticed the pattern and came after them. Slowly, each pack turned against the others. We lost many great people in that war. The men in those packs didn't think it was right what they were doing, but they

ZETA

were following their leader blindly. That made them cause many people a lot of irreparable damage."

He takes a second to get a cigarette. I wait to keep listening to what he has to say.

"We did what we had to do to survive. Day after day, we realized who we really were," Marcus says as the smoke rises and dissipates.

"Who were the packs that ignited the war? Was it Julius's crazy father?" I ask, intrigued.

He takes a drag off the cigarette, taking his time to answer. He finally exhales, looking at me, maybe wondering if it is proper to answer the question. "It was the Panther and Bear packs," he says with disappointment in his voice.

I can't believe it.

"I was barely starting, when the leader of the Panthers decided he wanted more. He convinced the Bear pack to join forces. They took it upon themselves to go against everyone else. We even took down other packs. When everything was happening, we knew what it meant for everyone else, and we never bothered to protect Miles and Kristov. We did as we were told, and that was our excuse to sleep well at night. That war left us all with a lot of horrible memories."

"What happened?" I ask without thinking he might not want to talk about it.

"In the end, we lost. A lot of people died. Relationships were affected, and we all continued to live with what we had done. The Bear and Panther packs were taken down. Most of them died. Gilligan and I survived because Miles stuck his neck out for us. Afterward, no pack wanted us to be part of them. Most of the others who survived decided to work honest jobs

VANTABLACK

and go on with life. Miles kept us under his protection after everything. We couldn't be Wolves, but he wanted to keep us safe. He helped us get back on our feet, and we were always in his debt. We never helped the Wolves; we helped Miles. He never gave up on us, so we never gave up on him."

He finishes his cigarette. We sit there in silence. I had no idea all of that had happened, most of it before I was born or when I was too young to remember any of it.

As we sit there, one of the men we sent to the Elephant pack walks in. He has news for us. He says the colonel has agreed to help us fight this war. We turn to look at each other. I send the man back to tell the other packs to be ready by the time the lights are on tomorrow, and we will brief everyone on the plan at the meeting place. Marcus and I keep thinking of the best way to end it all. We come up with a plan that hopefully will result in the fewest casualties.

It takes us a while to find a way to involve everyone in the plan. Everyone will assume the same level of risk; that way, no one will try to back out at the last minute. It takes us a while, and by the time we are done, it is late, so we decide to rest for tomorrow. We will wake up early, and we need to be prepared. We are going to try to end it all tomorrow if everything goes smoothly, but we also have to be prepared in case we have to fight for longer than that.

I make my way to bed and lie there in the dark. I don't close the door all the way. The door lets in a small strip of light coming from outside the room. I stare at the ceiling, trying to think of everything that has happened and trying not to think at all. I am worried. I

ZETA

haven't mentioned it to anyone, but I have been feeling anger inside myself. Sadness and a lust for revenge for what has happened.

When Marcus, Gilligan, and I attacked those people in the street, I felt my body differently. I felt as if my body were moving on its own, and I was just there watching it all happen. I don't want to mention it, because I think I am imagining something that is only happening in my mind. I feel lost, and now everyone is going to follow me into a battle. Something happened down there while I was gone. I am sure of it. The worst is that I keep trying to convince myself it isn't true.

A tear runs down from my eye without my realizing it. Eleonore walks in with a hot beverage for me. She holds it with two hands as she explains that it will help me sleep better. I sit up to grab the cup from her hands. She notices the tear running down my cheek, while I still haven't noticed it.

"Is everything all right?" she asks in a gentle voice.

I can tell she has been crying recently. I answer with a nod. She is not happy with my answer. Miles told me about Eleonore when we talked. She always wants to help, and she always keeps asking until she gets the answer that will tell her what the problem is. She asks again, and I give her the same answer. She stares at me for a second. I take a sip as we both wait for something to fill the silence.

"You know, Miles always talked with me about the things that bothered him. Maybe you could talk to Shanti when all of this is over. Maybe talking about it will help a little—not a lot but enough to get you away from the edge of your mind."

Her words hit close to home; I am feeling at the edge

VANTABLACK

right now. It seems she knows what she needs to say to get close. She probably said the same things to Miles to get him talking when he was being a hardhead. After all, she spent many years with him.

I turn and look her in the eye. It takes me a second to get the first word out, but after that, everything else comes rushing out. I tell her I feel different. My feelings are turning into something that worries me. I tell her what happened with the Snake group we took down and how it feels to be a passenger in my own body. It is hard to explain, but I also feel faster and stronger, as if all I have to do is think of what I want to do, and my body will move to do it faster and more efficiently than before. I tell her I lost myself in a dark place while I was away, and I feel I am not quite out of the darkness yet. Sometimes I feel I do not want to leave.

I try to put what I am feeling inside into words, but I find it difficult. I cannot find a way to explain or show her. I do the best I can.

I tell her I do not feel like myself, as if I have entered a new place inside myself that I never knew existed. The words keep coming out of my mouth. Eleonore listens in silence, staring at me. I assume I have already lost her in my attempt to explain. She never interrupts, and she makes me feel acknowledged.

I tell her, "I feel numb sometimes to everything around me. I can't feel anything at all at times, even when I try as hard as I can. Seeing Shanti made me feel again but only while I was around her. It seems it is easier for me to feel sadness and anger than other emotions. I cannot see any connection between the way I feel and how my body seems to feel sharper and stronger than before. I feel a connection between one

ZETA

thing and the other, but it is impossible to see the line that binds them together."

She listens to me for almost thirty minutes as I go on and on, trying to make sense of the hieroglyphics painted on the walls of the labyrinth inside my head.

After I am done, she takes a deep breath, probably confused by my words. I know if it were the other way around, I would be lost in trying to make sense of someone else's thoughts. I do not expect much of an answer, but now she knows. I know she would've kept thinking about it if I did not answer, so I've tried to put her mind at ease. Now, as I sit in silence with her, I wonder if I have made it worse. She probably does not know what the problem is, even after my explaining it, and does not know how to help me with what I am going through internally.

She smiles at me and looks me in the eye. "It's incredible that you say that. Miles told me something similar when we were younger, back when he had to fight before he became the leader of the Wolves. He tried explaining what he was feeling, but he found it hard to put into words. He felt he was all alone even when he was surrounded by people. He couldn't feel the love from everyone around him. It was easier for him to feel negative feelings than to embrace the ones that mattered. Miles said he felt anger most of the time. He was scared because he had no idea what was making him angry. He said he felt the anger and rage vanish only when he was fighting. If I remember correctly, he said, 'I'm scared that something vile inside me has taken over, helping me in my most barbaric moments, screaming to be let out so it can slay my enemies without giving them a chance. I'm scared it

VANTABLACK

will consume me, making me wither everything around me.' He sometimes told me he felt that he was going to end up all alone."

She tilts her head back to stop the tears from flowing. "One time, he told me he had always felt he was going to die either young or alone. When he told me that, I said to him, 'I'm not going anywhere. I will stay with you until the day you walk away from me.' I can only assume he died young because I wouldn't leave."

A tear comes rushing down her cheek. She hasn't noticed, but her words are helping. I feel that Miles went through something similar to what I am going through. If someone else could learn to live with this, maybe I can too.

"If you are going through the same things Miles went through, then I'm sorry for what I'm going to say next." Eleonore wipes her tear.

I want to know what she is going to tell me. Maybe it will serve as a guideline for me when I get to the kinds of moments Miles went through.

"You will begin to feel less as time passes. Most of the time, you will only feel negative emotions, if you are lucky enough not to feel numb constantly. You will love Shanti even when you begin to forget what love feels like. Unable to feel other people's embraces, love, and affection, you will treat them as they present themselves. You will become a kindhearted person unable to look away when those in need ask for help. You will try to save the world and every person in it. There will be times when you give everything to help others, and it will break you when they tell you they never asked for it, because they will be right. You will do all this to try to feel a connection to everyone else,

151

ZETA

because deep down, the bad things you have done in life will outweigh the good ones by a million. You'll always feel like a bad person who does not belong anywhere, as if your whole life is some cruel joke that never gets to the end. It will seem as if you are trying to buy yourself a place in heaven, knowing you will not get to enter. A voice in your head will always tell you that whatever you do is not enough."

"You will have to find a way to control the rage and use it for good. Sometimes you will feel as if you are trying to buy a ticket into heaven, and other times, you'll feel as if you are trying to buy your emotions back. It won't matter, because it will never be enough, but that will make you a person with a kind heart willing to save others even when they wouldn't do the same. You will be a hero in the eyes of those you protect and a villain in the eyes of your enemies. You will be a hero, although you won't ever feel like it. The good things you do will never make you feel better. They will come and go like a breeze, without stopping for you to appreciate their presence, but you won't be able to stop doing them. The darkness you see inside yourself will make you try to hold the flame that guides others, even if it burns you."

She grabs on to her shirt with a fist, fighting the tears. I don't know if I am going to go through that kind of life, but it gives me some relief to know that maybe those I help will see me that way instead of the way I see myself.

"Miles went through that. He died so others could live. I wonder if his last thought was 'Was I good enough?'"

I place a hand over hers. She places her other hand over mine and smiles at me. She hugs me for a moment.

152

VANTABLACK

Afterward, she pulls away, telling me to finish my drink so I can sleep better, and then she walks out of the room. I sit there drinking, lost in my head. I finish the drink, and I lie back in bed, wondering if my biggest enemy will always be my mind. Is it a good thing or a bad thing to have your enemy living inside your head, always engaged in a never-ending battle? I think it is a good thing because that way, no one else can ever hurt me like I hurt myself. I think it is a bad thing because I can never let my guard down, or I will hurt myself.

Is it good or bad? I think as I drift away into sleep.

Thirteen

I wake up the next morning. Eleonore is already up, and so are most of the men who are going to help us in the fight. Everyone has already eaten, and now they are getting their gear ready and waiting for Marcus and me. I sit at the table with Eleonore, eating breakfast. Marcus hasn't made it to the table yet. I feel different this morning after the conversation I had with Eleonore last night. I thank her for listening to me, and she tells me she hopes it helped, even if just a little. It did. Maybe knowing what I am going to get hit with in life makes it easier for me to digest what is going on in my head.

"Now, when all of this is over, you will have Shanti to talk to. Just like Miles had me. It will be hard at first, but if you do not want to lose her, it's best if you let her in. It will help you both grow together, taking some weight off your chest, and it will help her to know what is happening. Communication will help you both, like it did with us." She holds my hand with a smile.

I am glad I have Shanti with me. We are all going to do our best to end the chaos today. We are all going to fight to regain our peace. I drift away to memories of Shanti, thinking about how we would walk and converse while holding hands. Maybe we can do that again once this is all over. I just want to be able to hold her again

VANTABLACK

without having to let her go. It will all come down to this battle. The winners will dictate the future in the bunker.

Marcus walks in. He has two swords with him. He lays one next to me and grabs something to drink. Eleonore wants to give him a plate of food, but he only wants an apple.

"That's your sword for the battle," Marcus says. "I had one of the guys bring it down here for you from the remains of the old building."

I open it. It is beautiful—a black Japanese-style sword. It seems it has seen some fights before, but it is still in great condition.

Eleonore gives him his apple and then turns to look at me as I go over every detail of the sword. "That's a good sword," she says with a smile. "Miles's predecessor used to love it."

It is one of the elders' swords. Miles must have had it stashed away.

"Miles had Gilligan and me work on that sword. He wanted you to have it. It's the sword the leader of the Wolves wielded back when Miles arrived," Marcus says.

It is a great sword, made from a strong material that is extremely light too. It also has space for modules to be added for fighting.

I stand up and thank Eleonore for the food. Marcus grabs his sword from the table and gives Eleonore a hug. "We will bring his sword back for you," Marcus whispers to her.

We walk outside, where everyone is gathered. They are going to follow us to meet with the other packs and the Elephants, so we can inform everyone of the plan. We start walking, covering ourselves, avoiding detection

ZETA

from the Snake pack. We do not want them to notice we are getting ready for a fight.

We all gather around the market. By the time we get there, the Elephants have already cleared the Snakes in the area and started a perimeter. Not long after, the Apes appear. They have brought with them Gilligan, who stayed with them after the delivery. He walks over to Marcus and me, and we greet him with a hug.

He informs us that King has let Vultures join him to fight. They saw our men make the food deliveries. After everyone ate, they heard a knock on the door. It was a huge crowd; at first, they thought it was the Snakes, but they noticed the crowd did not have any weapons. One of them walked forward and asked for food. King didn't know if he should oblige, but Gilligan advised him that he should; there was plenty of food left to go around. After they ate, the Vultures wanted to repay them, and without King or Gilligan having to ask, the Vultures told them they wanted to fight by their side. They too want to end the purge the Snakes have started.

We are happy the Snakes don't have such a big group on their side. I had no idea this many Vultures lived on every level of the bunker.

The Fox pack arrive at the gathering point. Zack has brought Shanti with him. As they make their way, everyone takes notice of something odd happening: one after another, the Vultures look at Shanti and smile at her, putting their closed fists near their hearts. Some of them even cry. They must know her or remember all the years she's spent trying to feed them one by one. Not all of them know her, but they all know about her.

She leaves Zack's side to go hug a woman who is looking at her with open arms. Shanti walks up to her

VANTABLACK

and gives her a hug. The woman thanks her, as do some of the other men and women who have encountered her before.

Gilligan, Marcus, and I walk toward the center of the marketplace. Zack is the first one to gather there with us.

"Why did you bring Shanti?" I ask.

"She wanted to come see you before we left. She told me she was going to come see you whether I allowed her to or not, so I decided to escort her. She was going to do what she wanted either way," Zack says.

We both laugh. I turn to look at her. She's still being praised by the Vultures who have joined the Apes in the fight.

The colonel and King join us soon after. We explain the plan.

"We will have men covering every entrance and exit on this level as the rest of us hunt the Snake pack. We will go through each street until we clear them off on this level. Once we have eliminated all of them from here, we will move on to the next level until it's clear. We won't let anyone in or out until it's clear," Marcus says.

"Covering the exits to lower and upper levels will help us stay in control of detection. The Snakes on the other levels won't know we are coming, and they won't be able to alert each other. That way, they won't have a chance to prepare for an attack or go into hiding," I add.

"Good plan. Simple but good," says the colonel.

"Why do it like this? Why not just hunt them down and keep cornering them until they all end up in one place and then destroy them all together?" King asks.

"If we went about it like that, they could run to a level above or below, making us divide. Aside from that,

ZETA

we would all just be running around slaying people without any coordination or plan. That would mean more casualties, and some of them might get away," the colonel says.

"We decided to go with this plan so everyone's pack has the same level of exposure and threat as everyone else's. No one is left to take the hit more than others, and we get to take the enemy by surprise," I say.

"This works. I assume we still have no word of where Kristov or Julius is, right? So this will help us search and hunt at the same time," Zack says.

Everyone seems to be on the same page after being briefed. We order groups of our men to go guard the exits and entrances of this level. As I explain to some of our men what to do, Gilligan taps me on the shoulder. I look at him, and he points me toward Shanti with a head movement.

I walk away, and Gilligan continues to brief them. Shanti stands smiling at me as I walk toward her.

"You were not going to leave again without saying goodbye, right?" she asks jokingly.

I hug her and hold her close. She kisses me. I feel at peace with her, even when we are about to finish a war.

She pulls away after kissing me, leaving me wanting more. She has to go, as we are about to begin. War waits for no love. As she walks away, she turns and says, "Please come back to me."

Zack orders some of his best men to take her back into the Fox building to keep her safe. I watch her disappear in the distance.

Everyone runs to his position. Zack walks next to me as says, "Don't worry, lover boy; she will be waiting for you when all this is over." Gilligan and Marcus hear

VANTABLACK

him and laugh. I just smile, trying to hold on to the happiness she gave me in those few seconds.

Once we leave the market, we advance in the streets, looking for the Snake pack. Ashes still cover the streets, moving around as our men, walking fast, look for their target. Sometimes it is easy to spot them, as they have their emblem on their skin or clothing. Some of them are creating chaos in the streets, killing or torturing people. We slay them one by one or in groups; it doesn't really matter.

It is clear the madness of their leaders is ingrained in them, so we decide to put them out of their misery. It is easy not to see them as human anymore, as we see the atrocities they have done to those too weak to fight back and the smiles on their faces as they annihilate the people they once walked among not long ago.

All around the streets on this level, I can hear swords colliding. Some of the Snakes have good weapons to fight back. Others have only their fists and whatever they can find to use as a weapon. It isn't fair for some of them, but if it were the other way around, they wouldn't stop to think about it. With this many people with us, it doesn't take us long to clear this level. After a couple of hours, we gather at the entrances our men are guarding. Before we dismissed them from this world, some of the Snakes told us more of their men are on the levels above.

There are four exits and entrances in each wall of each level. After clearing one level, we use flares the colonel has provided to signal to one another that we are done. That way, nobody will go ahead and leave an opening for the enemy to escape or go around us.

Once a flare from each pack is lit, we all move to the

159

ZETA

next level and wait ten minutes to assess the injured or any casualties. Pausing also helps us to keep a count of the number of men we need to leave and keep on going.

We keep going, clearing level after level without any casualties. Sometimes a few are injured, but we send them back to the level we started on to get treated. As we pass each level, we see only Snake enemies. On every new level we reach, they seem to be more prepared and better equipped to fight.

After a couple of levels, we reach the Snakes who have swords and crossbows with modifications to them. Some of the swords are able to heat up without breaking. Other swords are covered in fire or poison. Some of them drip acid or emit electricity. It is the same way with the crossbows. It is difficult but not impossible to defeat them. We are just glad they don't have any guns.

Slowly, the more inexperienced fighters start to get injured or killed. After many levels, our numbers are decreasing, with casualties being mostly Vultures following the Apes or civilians fighting among the Elephants.

We take longer to advance when we reach the harder levels. The Snakes don't have more men throughout these levels, but they now know we're coming for them, and there are traps in some areas. On the higher levels, there aren't as many Snake groups, but these men are stronger and harder to defeat. We all do our best to avoid being killed or injured. Most of our men still fighting have minimal cuts and bruising, and they are getting tired. I keep going without a problem, but as I look around me, I see that the others are having a hard time catching their breath, even Marcus and Gilligan. I can't do this alone, so we rest.

VANTABLACK

The day is almost gone, and we are proud of the progress we have made. We send a few men to tell the other groups to rest, and we will continue in the morning. We decide to rest on the last level we have cleared, sending men to gather food and water before the lights go out. We eat, and then we rest in shifts. When my turn to rest comes, the lights are still out on the street, but when I open my eyes again, it is already light out.

Those of us resting at the time are woken by the people around us starting a discussion. When I rise from the floor where I have been sleeping, I see several explosions in the distance. They are coming from the wall the Elephant pack is covering so nobody will come in or out. I order everyone to stay put as I run as fast as I can. Marcus and Gilligan yell for me to stay, but I have to make sure nothing has ruined our plan.

As I run toward the commotion, I worry that someone might make it across the Elephant line and alert Julius and Kristov. Julius is a smart enemy I am not going to make the mistake of underestimating twice in my life. We still have no idea where they are hiding. We have advanced as much as we can, but I fear we are not even close to the end of this. I promised myself I would end this today, and I have failed. Our men are going down slowly. At this rate, we will reach the top with only a handful of men by our side to fight. The way the enemy has positioned themselves to cover so many levels with so few men makes me think Julius is advising Kristov or has already taken over the Snake pack. There is no way Kristov would let Julius throw all his men into the grinder that easily.

When I finally reach the Elephant-guarded area, fire

ZETA

is spreading slowly. The Elephant pack is on one side, and a few men from the Snake pack are on the opposite side. No one is moving. I wonder what has caused all the damage in the streets.

Out of nowhere, I see the colonel in the middle, with his uniform coat torn. He is fighting someone. I have never seen the person before. I can tell it is an incredibly strong enemy. The two of them seem to have been fighting for a while. I wonder why the colonel does not let his men help him finish this fight. I turn to see where his men are standing. Some of them seem to have been recently injured. The colonel must have thought they would only get themselves killed and decided to take matters into his own hands.

The colonel and his enemy are both breathing heavily. They are not giving each other any time to breathe more than they need to. Their swords collide. I can hear the metal scream. No one dares to enter the battle area. If anyone not on their level tried to compete with them, he would be torn to pieces. I know that leaders are strong in fights, but I had no idea they had this level of strength.

I swear they are pushing hot air all around them with every swing of their swords. It seems the colonel is fighting with some anger. He must be mad because of the damage his enemy has done to his men.

The enemy swings his sword, cutting the colonel's skin. The colonel doesn't flinch. He just keeps going. I can't tell if he is ignoring the pain or if he doesn't feel it at this point. They keep trying to kill each other, and no one can do anything about it. The swords seem as if they are going to break with each strike, but they never do.

VANTABLACK

They both swing their swords as hard as they can. I see sparks flying off. They stay there, pushing each other with their swords, for a second. The colonel strikes his enemy by headbutting him. With a kick, he pushes him back. His enemy takes a few steps backward, holding his stomach.

The colonel takes a deep breath. The enemy activates the modification in his sword. It is acid. The enemy sword catches a light green florescent color. The enemy rushes the colonel. He doesn't move from the place where he stands.

The enemy swings his sword, splashing some of the acid around everywhere. Some acid drops fly in the colonel's direction. One lands on his clothing. When the enemy gets close enough to strike, the colonel lets out the air he has been holding. He steps to the side, avoiding being hit. He strikes the enemy with his fist as hard as he can, putting him on the ground. With his other hand, he holds the sword, striking as hard as he can at the floor where the enemy lies. The enemy tries to cover himself from the blow, but it is no use. The colonel uses all his strength, breaking the enemy's sword on contact. The acid falls onto him, burning him. He would scream, but the blow has struck his chest, hitting his heart. The enemy is dead before the acid touches his skin.

"Those of you who have rested, take care of the rest," the colonel says as he swings his sword down to remove the lingering remains of blood and acid.

The enemies, upon seeing their ally fall, run in fear. A handful of the men standing behind the colonel run to get them. Not long after, the screams of the enemies being struck down and killed can be heard. The colonel

ZETA

walks back to the area where he was resting before the fight.

I follow him. I want to ask him about the fight he just had. He sits as one of his men assesses him for any major damage he might have received. He sits there drinking and eating. I walk closer to him.

"How is it that you can fight with such strength?" I ask.

I am worried the next enemies will be the same. I can fight for long periods of time, more than most, but I am worried about the strength with which they were exchanging blows. I have never received a hit as brutal as the ones they were exchanging, and I am sure I cannot take one on at full speed and be conscious afterward.

"You just do. I'm surprised you thought much of that. The way Miles spoke of you, I was sure you could go toe to toe with the best. Maybe he was wrong about you." The colonel keeps eating after he answers me.

"Is there special training, or did you do something to fight that way? Why would Miles speak of me with you?" I have a million questions.

"Relax, kid. There's not much to say. Miles and I kept in communication from time to time. After a while of your working for him, he started taking notice of what you did. I remember he spoke highly of you. And my men sometimes ran into people you used to fight when you were running about in the bunker. Most of them were almost dying when we found them after they picked fights with you."

I had no idea the colonel knew so much about me. I always thought I covered my tracks well enough.

"When you fight, does your body get stiff?" he asks.

VANTABLACK

I shake my head.

"Do you pull back after throwing a hit or try to slow your hit down as if it is losing power?" He leans forward as he asks.

I nod slowly.

"When you fight, what do you feel? Do you fight as if there is water all around you? Or does it feel like you are fighting in a dream, and it feels hard to hit your target?"

I take a second to answer. "My body starts to feel warm, as if a fire has started in my chest, and I hold it there. My body feels like it's surrounded by water as I release vapors from my skin. I have never been able to go all in." I look down at the ground.

"That's interesting. Usually, it's one way or another with this thing but never so many things at once. Miles used to be the same way; he had more than one feeling going on as he fought. The only advice I can give you that works with one of the feelings you have is to let the fire in your chest spread. Let it flow through your limbs as if it is your own blood flowing. Maybe you can figure out the other ones on your own. I don't know how Miles did it."

"Miles could fight like you?" I ask.

"You never saw Miles fight all out? Well, that's no surprise; there are very few contenders here who can fight like that. If he'd fought with any normal person, he would have probably killed the person without breaking a sweat. Miles was good. I was never able to take him on and win. He wouldn't fight with all strength like me. He was more of a calculating adversary. Marcus and I always told him Julius was probably one of the only ones who could go against him and give a show. He never cared. Marcus always felt Julius would be trouble

165

ZETA

one way or another, but Miles just wanted to live in peace. Righteous Miles—that's what the other kids called him to make fun of him when we were growing up. He saw some of that in you, among other things. What I wouldn't give to be able to spar with him again. That would be something else. I guess I could spar with Marcus or Gilligan, but I don't think they could give me the freedom Miles gave me when we went at it." He stops to take a sip of his drink.

"Marcus and Gilligan can fight like that?" I ask, amazed.

"Absolutely. I'm surprised you haven't seen them yet. Those bastards must be holding back for the higher levels. King, Julius, and Kristov too. Zack might be able to; I don't know how much Tobaqui trained him for. You do not become the leader of anything by being like everyone else, kid. People don't want to follow someone who is like them. They want to follow someone who can inspire them and show them a glimpse of greatness, even if just for a second, and fuel them with his words and give them a reason to get back up after they are down. If you try to lead and can't bring greatness with you, someone else will put you down, and that will be the end of your time as a leader."

I can see his words fueling the men within earshot. He is able to bring that fire from inside them without realizing it.

"Now, go on, boy, back to your pack. I need some rest if we are to finish this thing as soon as possible. Can't fight beside a tired soldier."

I smile as he turns away and heads off to take a nap. I make my way in the darkness back to the pack. I think of what he said to me. I have never thought of a way

VANTABLACK

to help my body fight better. I've always assumed that I fought the best way my body could and that it would get better in time. I have to pay more attention to how my body feels and moves. I have to place myself on the same level they are on if I am going to see this mission through to the end.

Fourteen

The next morning, we send people to gather food for the ones who are still fighting. Everyone eats before heading into the level and clearing it out.

We continue clearing area after area. I decide to take a step back to watch Gilligan and Marcus fight. I notice it is easy for them to slay their enemies. At times, they see someone having trouble fighting back and step in to help. Their skill makes them untouchable. After a few levels, they begin to slow down a little. I guess skill is a good thing to have, but they aren't as young as they once were. I keep forgetting they are older than I am. Even as they grow tired, they are still miles ahead of their adversaries. My talk with the colonel last night has made me realize their skill, something I didn't pay attention to before. To me, they have always been my friends, shopkeepers who fix things for the Wolf pack and overprice their services to people they don't like. It's weird how certain circumstances can make you see people you have known almost your whole life in a different light.

Marcus and Gilligan notice I have been letting them carry the weight as I watch them and try to assess their strength. They give me smiles, making fun of me for being surprised at my sudden realization. After that, I

VANTABLACK

decide to help. I can't let them finish this by themselves. They would never let me hear the end of it.

We keep clearing level after level, slowly losing men. I have forgotten how many levels are in this bunker. It has been so long since I have been this high up.

We have almost finished clearing the level we are on. Our men are spread thin. I can see some of the men from the Ape pack being led by King a couple of streets away. Zack and his group are not far behind. All of us reach the center. There aren't many men to clear, but we still have to take on a few here and there. I see the colonel keep swinging his sword, putting enemies down, and his team finishes them off. He reaches the center of the level before any of us.

When the rest of us finally catch up, we find the colonel fighting multiple enemies at once. They are strong too. They are all surrounding one building, ready to fight.

Could this be it? The place where Julius and Kristov are hiding? I think.

Our troops are still catching up to us. We decide to lower the enemy numbers by giving them a fight. The colonel takes on as many enemies as he can at once. He isn't holding back one bit. I can hear his sword cutting the air around him. I look at Marcus and Gilligan as they rush into action. Their intensity grows. I can see by the way they are fighting that they are in a hurry to end everyone trying to stop us from entering the building.

I rush behind them, trying to reduce the enemy's numbers as much as I can so our men with less experience have a higher chance of survival. While I fight, I see glimpses of the others around me.

Zack has joined the fight. Even with only one arm,

169

ZETA

he seems unstoppable. He must have trained hard with the old Fox pack leader. I can see why they chose him. He might have lost his arm, but they can't take away the threat level he is in battle. I have never seen him fight before, but I have heard from others that he is a beast, as a leader should be.

I have heard that King enjoys fighting. He seems to be dancing and playing as he takes on as many as the colonel. He taunts them and dares them to attack him. King has raw power like the colonel's, but I can see he does not know how to control it or even hold back. It is hard to tell if he does not know how to hold back or does not want to. For him, fighting is nothing more than a show.

By the time the troops in each group arrive, there aren't many enemies left. Only a few strong-looking enemies remain at the door, stopping us from rushing in. Our troops surround the building.

We can't just run into the building. Who knows how many more men are inside, if there are any?

"I don't need to go in. You need to come out!" I hear someone yell.

I turn to see who said it—Zack. One of his men hands him a Molotov. Before anyone can say anything, we see it fly through the air toward its destination. It hits the building. Immediately, many more start flying. The Fox pack throw them at the building one after another but avoid hitting the entrance.

Flames engulf the building. Soon after, the men hiding inside come rushing out. There aren't as many as I expect. Everyone's troops begin to fight. I can hear the resentment in their hearts. Their actions scream for justice. There is chaos in the entrance of the building.

VANTABLACK

I see the colonel rush in. He starts swinging his sword, throwing enemies away from his path, creating a clear area around himself. He has spotted Kristov coming out. King, Zack, Marcus, and Gilligan see him too. Everyone runs toward him. I follow.

The colonel is on the offensive, and Kristov can't do much but deflect his massively strong charges.

"Why, Kristov? Why?" the colonel yells as he keeps attacking him.

Kristov won't give an answer. Surrounded by enemies, he still has a crazy smile.

Zack is dying to jump into the fight. King only watches, just as Gilligan and I do. Marcus is holding his sword with a tight grip. He must want to take him on too.

Kristov and the colonel swing their swords at each other. When the blades collide, it feels as if they are about to break from the impact. They both take a step back.

"Where's Julius, Kristov? Let's get this over with already," King says.

"As you can see, he isn't here," he answers without losing sight of the colonel.

"We just want to put an end to this. Let us know where he is, and we can close this chapter. It's not like you can get away from us now," Gilligan says.

"You decided to be part of his plan and killed possibly the last person who ever cared about you. Was it worth it?" the colonel says.

I can see Marcus is getting more amped up with every second that passes. He wants to let loose against Kristov. We need the location of Julius before anybody kills him.

171

ZETA

The colonel's words seem to sting Kristov, even if for just a second. I can see in his face that there is some truth to what the colonel has just said to him. Marcus sees it too.

"The one man who was always on your side, no matter how badly you screwed up. You took advantage of the fact that he would never raise his sword to kill you, and you allowed Julius to cut him down. You raised your sword and killed him, knowing he could never harm you, even when he wanted to!" Marcus exclaims with disgust.

"What did he offer you, Kristov? What was Miles's life worth to you?" the colonel asks in a calm voice. "Where is your last friend in the world now?"

"He's not my friend!" Kristov finally lets out an answer. Everyone stays silent, hoping he will keep talking. He does. "He promised me half the bunker and said he would take over the other half. He took over the top, and I kept the rest. After we burned the first level down, we threw everyone else left from the other levels into the chaos to sort themselves out. We allowed some to join us." He looks around, still holding his sword in front of him, guarding himself. "After we took over the other levels, I decided to pay him a visit. All the upper levels were completely empty. We followed him to the top floor. When we got there, his people wouldn't allow us to see him. They were ready to fight us if we tried. He sent one of his men to tell me I had completed my usefulness. He knew you all would come to kill me at some point, and so did I. He devised this whole plan, and I still don't know why. All I know is that he couldn't take you all out, so he left me behind so we could kill each other."

172

VANTABLACK

"Don't worry; after we are done with you, we will deal with him too. Now, be a good boy, and point to where he is hiding," King says mockingly.

"Didn't you just hear me? He is right above us. The top level of the bunker. He planned all this. Every step, every turn, and all the outcomes to stop us from reaching him. There's something up there he wants," Kristov says desperately.

"He did not plan this very well. As you can see, we are just one level short of ending this," Zack says as he extends his sword, pointing it toward Kristov.

I look up. I had no idea we'd climbed this far up. I can't remember how many levels we have gone through. One more level up, past all the concrete and lights above, Julius is waiting for us.

"Don't get cocky, kid. That's what made me take your arm off the last time," Kristov says, taunting Zack.

Zack takes a step forward. King is able to stop him before he takes another one. That is what Kristov wants. Zack gives him a smile to let him know he is coming for him.

"You guys still think you are going to win. You still can't see that Julius is more than one step ahead of you. Let me guess: you guys don't have that many fighters anymore. Depleted most of your troops to make it to me, only to find out there's a little bit more to go. Almost at the finish line. So many injured you probably sent them back to get better." Kristov pauses for a second and turns to Zack. His insane smile comes back. "If there are only weak men on the other levels and all the strong ones are here, how many men do you think it would take to drag Shanti away from the Fox pack?"

173

ZETA

Zack launches at him. I turn around and try to run away from everyone. Gilligan stops me.

Kristov says, "Where do you think you are going? What makes you think they haven't already taken her? You can't make all this noise on level after level and expect nobody to notice. If you hadn't rested for one night, maybe you would have made it there before they got her."

I want to run, but I have no idea where I should go. Zack can't get past King.

"If I've got it right, Shanti is just about to be delivered to Julius as we speak, but don't worry. That level has no buildings at all; it's just a floor all the way around, which means you won't have to waste time searching for Julius. All you have to do is get past his men, and you can save her. So here's the choice for you heroes: you can stay here and finish fighting us, or you can go try to make it in time to save Shanti. Take my word for it: you are going to need every last able soldier you've got to take him down."

"Oh yeah? Why is that?" the colonel asks.

"Because all the way to this point, you have only fought the civilians who joined us to survive and my men from the Snakes. Julius has not taken a single loss this whole time. I doubt you have enough men to fight, but I'm rooting for you," Kristov says.

I turn to look at Zack. He gives me a nod, letting me know he has this under control. "Bring her back. We will be with you shortly. I just need to cut his head off before I go. We can still make it. Take your men, and go," Zack says as he turns away.

I run toward the closest stairway to reach the next level. Marcus and Gilligan follow close behind me,

VANTABLACK

yelling to the rest of our men, "On me!" They follow us into the unknown.

Everyone else stays behind to fight. The Wolves follow us as we make our way up the stairs. The number of entrances is greatly reduced: I notice there are only six entrances to the highest level. The doorways are tall, all on the same side of the bunker. When we finally arrive, the lights blind us for a second. I keep running as others slow down, trying to cover their eyes.

When I am able to make out what is in front of me, I see a small group of men walking away from our direction. The one in the back is holding Shanti by the arm and pulling her to follow.

I look in the direction they are walking. The Tiger pack men are at the opposite end of this level, which seems significantly smaller than all the other levels in the bunker. The group of men is large, and they seem to be working on something in one specific area. The men who have abducted Shanti are closer to us than they are to their destination.

The Tigers at the end make way for a man to stand out among them. It's Julius. He notices the group he sent to capture Shanti, and then he realizes we are close behind them. The group of men take notice of Julius staring at something past them, and they turn around to look. They stop and stare as they smile victoriously. The men behind Julius keep working. It seems they are piling something against a wall. The wall doesn't look like the other walls of the bunker.

Julius smiles from ear to ear. He turns around to say something to his men. They all continue to move as they did before they took notice of us. The men escorting Shanti have not moved from their place yet.

175

ZETA

I slow down as I move toward them and then stop. The others walk up beside me. I have a bad feeling. I turn to look at Marcus and Gilligan. There is uncertainty in their faces. What is Julius planning? Kristov's words about how smart Julius is echo in my head. I can't afford to doubt myself, not with this much on the line. No one moves. We all stand here looking at one another.

I try to come up with a way to narrow the gap between the abductors and myself. If I can get close enough to them to grab Shanti, I am sure I can take her to a safe place. Julius has not made a move against us yet; he stands there looking at us as if he has all the time in the world. I try to think like him, trying to make out what he has planned, but I draw a blank. Time keeps passing by, and no one moves a muscle, aside from the men standing behind Julius, who have completely disregarded our existence.

It is infuriating to see Shanti in this position and not be able to help her without putting her at risk. Is he playing with me? Is it part of his plan to see how much I am willing to take to ensure she is safe? Or is he buying time? It seems odd that he hasn't ordered them to deliver her to him already. I feel he is playing with me, taunting me with her. What can I do? I scream in my mind, trying to find a solution but unable to find one.

It feels like an eternity as we wait here. Suddenly, we hear steps coming from behind us. Gilligan turns around to see who it is. I choose not to, fearing that Julius might try to do something in the split second I take to turn around.

"It's the others. Some of them finally caught up," Gilligan says.

I am incapable of moving. Is it fear of the situation

or fear of the repercussions that will come if I do move? Either way, I cannot take any chances. I am at the mercy of Julius as long as he has Shanti to threaten me with. It is up to him to make the first move. Or so I think.

I can hear steps running up to us from behind. I don't bother to turn around; I just assume they will slow down when they get to where we are. They don't.

The steps keep going long past us. At first, all I see is a shadow. Then the shadow takes the form of the back of a person's body. I realize it is Zack running toward his sister. I turn to look at Shanti as she cries, unable to set herself free. I turn my gaze to Julius, who wears a smile different from the one he has been showing us the whole time we have been waiting here.

I have been waiting for him to make a move. It never occurred to me he already has. He is waiting for a counteraction, but it is not mine. He isn't battling me at all. I am just a piece in the plan he created. I thought I was his opponent, but that is not true. He has created this scenario for someone else. He knows exactly how his target will react, causing all the chips to fall into place for him. It takes me a second to figure this out now that all the pieces are in front of me, and it is too late for me to alert Zack.

My heart beats faster and faster until I can no longer feel my heartbeat at all. I can't feel a pause between each beat. Everything around me seems to slow down. I can see the way Julius has planned for this situation to unravel.

Zack reaches the men holding Shanti, and he tries to fight them all on his own. The rest of the Fox pack rush behind him, trusting their leader in his decision. Julius, at a distance, gives his men a signal. A few of them turn

ZETA

around, holding something in their hands. One of them hands Julius an item, which he holds with both hands.

Actions keep happening, but I hear no sound. Even as everyone screams and yells, there is complete silence as the events take place all around me. I can't hear anything; I am lucky enough to move as the chaos starts to unravel before our eyes.

Julius and four of his men pull out automatic guns. They point them in our direction and start firing without any regard for their men. Some of the men from the Fox pack are shot down. Those who are injured but still alive try to move, but they aren't strong enough. Julius fires at Zack and Shanti even with his men still in the line of fire. He doesn't care whom he has to take down as long as he is able to get what he wants. The Wolves run to opposite sides, trying to be lucky enough not to get hit by the bullets.

Julius shoots his men down, firing as he tries to get Zack. I see Shanti get hit by a bullet in the stomach and then another. She falls to the ground. I run toward her without thinking. I can only react to what is happening to her. The bullets are still flying all around us. Julius and his men reload and continue to fire. Zack is shot down, along with everyone from the Tiger pack who is around him.

The bullets fly everywhere as I run as fast as I can to reach Shanti. The floor around her is covered with blood. I wish this were not true but just another hallucination. I want to wake up again on the lowest level of the bunker, knowing this nightmare has all been in my mind.

I reach Shanti, and I fall to my knees. I grab her, raising her from the floor so she can sit up straight. I do not know what to do. She sees Zack lying there

VANTABLACK

lifeless. She begins to cry. She has been in shock this whole time.

I press on her wound in her stomach with one hand, trying to stop the blood rushing out. I know there is no point in doing so. I can feel my hand on her back dripping in her blood. I feel panic as everything around me crumbles in front of me. Shanti tries to pull my hand away from her stomach.

"No, Shanti. I must put pressure so you can stay with me. Okay?" I say as tears run down my face.

She is having a hard time breathing. She keeps gasping for air as she looks at me. She notices my tears as her body shakes, and her legs keep kicking. She moves my hand away from her wound as I stop applying pressure. We both know there is no stopping this. I look into her eyes. She wipes my tears with her hand, which has blood on it.

She smiles. I try to smile through the tears so she can see one more time how happy she makes me. The world disappears around us for the last time.

"You will be all right. This is part of life, to live and die. Do not die here with me. Leave, and please find a way to be happy. I wish you could see yourself the way I see you. Maybe that way, I could take those nightmares in your head with me. I love you."

Shanti lets out her last words as I hold her in my arms. She closes her eyes as she leaves this world. She seems to be asleep here in my arms. It takes me a second to realize she is gone. She is gone, and there is nothing I can do to change that.

"Please come back. Please stay. I need your light with me!" I hold her in my arms. "I came back to you.

ZETA

I am here. Please don't go. We can be together. I have you right here!"

I yell at the top of my lungs, pleading in vain for time to go backward and let me be with her. As she leaves my side, I find myself all alone. There is only darkness around me once again.

Faintly, I hear Marcus and Gilligan distantly calling for me. Their voices keep getting farther away from me. The bullets have stopped flying. I lay Shanti's body on the floor as I get back on my feet. I turn to my right to see Julius smiling with an empty gun in his hand.

Rage fills my heart and travels deeper to parts of me I didn't know I still had. Sinister and vile thoughts of all the things I can do to him fill my mind. I draw my sword and turn to get a good look at him.

You want him to pay, don't you? A familiar voice echoes in my head. I feel it getting closer. *He took away yet another light that was keeping you from the darkest parts inside yourself. How many more will you allow him to take? He isn't done yet, and you know that. It's just a matter of time until he wants to come for Eleonore, Marcus, Gilligan, and all the other Wolves. He has to be put down, and you know it.*

Everything around me is pitch black. The voice makes sense. I feel as if an animal wants to be let loose inside me. Maybe it is something worse.

I can help you end it. All you have to do is sit back and relax. See the show. What do you say, kid?

VANTABLACK

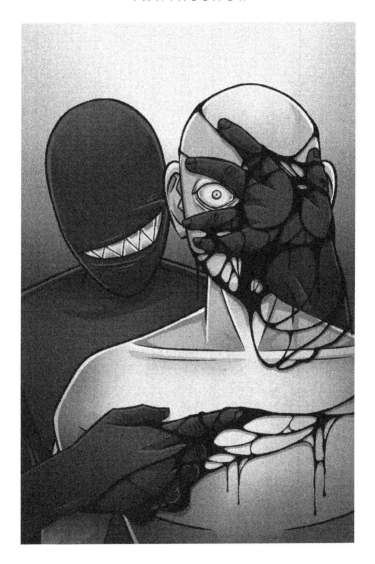

Julius smiles as he grabs his sword. Marcus and Gilligan run toward me from behind. I see Julius's smile disappear for a second as if in fear. I realize he is looking at me. Marcus and Gilligan catch up to me. They grab

ZETA

me and try to pull me away, but they can't. They walk up next to me, and their expressions change. There is a demonic smile painted on my face.

I am no longer in control of my body. There is something else fueling me. I wish I knew what it is.

I run toward Julius. The men behind him place themselves in front of him. Marcus, Gilligan, and everyone else who is still alive run behind me. They try to keep up, but my speed keeps increasing, widening the gap between us.

The next thing I know, I am face-to-face with the Tigers who stand between me and Julius. They swing their swords, trying to get me. I slay them before they realize I have already passed them. Their blood flies above us and then falls slowly like rain. I keep moving without being touched. They try their best, but it isn't enough.

As I keep moving forward, I see Julius little by little as the bodies keep falling down. He can't tell which side I am going to reach him on; he sees only the bodies of his men collapsing one after another all around him.

I finally reach him. My sword gains speed as it gets closer to him. He is able to block my attack at the last second. He flies backward from the blow. More of his men step in front of him to protect him. I can hear my allies catching up, already fighting the men I haven't killed yet.

Julius orders his men to go attack the rest of our troops. "What are you doing? Go take care of the others! I'll deal with him." They go around me to attack them, avoiding me and clearing a path for me to get to Julius.

A few of his men stay behind to finish what they are doing against the wall behind Julius. It seems they have

VANTABLACK

electronics stacked against it, along with explosives. I don't care; I am not here for that.

Julius takes his stance with his sword in both hands. He takes his first step, and I do the same. I am in front of him before he can notice. My speed keeps increasing. I swing my sword, but he is able to stop it at the last second.

I hear the colonel's voice in my head, repeating what he said about leaders being strong. Could Julius be as strong as the colonel? I just keep watching my body move itself, fighting like an animal with no choice of retreat.

Julius takes a deep breath and switches to offense. He pushes me back with the strength of each blow of our swords colliding. He smiles as if he is enjoying himself. He must think he can't lose. He keeps attacking. Was he taken by surprise by my first attacks?

He takes a wide step and swings his sword as he screams. His speed increases. He has more power behind him than I thought. I can't stop his attack, so I have to deflect it. He is able to create a small cut on my forehead. Every time he attacks me is an attempt to kill immediately. I can see that he has been doing this for a long time.

He swings again. I take a step to the side, avoiding his blade without being able to cut him down with mine. I punch him as hard as I can. He is pushed back. His smile doesn't disappear. He is bleeding from his mouth.

"I should have started this a long time ago. I've been waiting for someone to spar with. I would have liked to go against Miles, but you know, he had to be put down," Julius says, taunting me.

My rage grows, and I rush toward him. When I am

183

ZETA

about to reach him, he steps forward and punches me in the stomach. My body folds downward. *Such strength.* I roll to the side as he tries to cut me down as I grab my stomach. It is as if I can guess his next move.

Inside my head, I feel the darkness around me climbing upward, holding me prisoner. I can feel that it wants to keep control of my body forever and leave me no choice but to watch the world go by without being able to do anything. I try to fight it back as I stand up.

In that moment, Julius comes for me. He is able to cut some of my shirt with his swing; I am able to dodge it by jumping back as he follows. I have to fight Julius and whatever has taken over me at the same time. Julius takes advantage of the moments when I try to regain control of my body. I am able to stop him most of the time without getting injured.

"Come on now. Don't disappoint me, kid; give me everything you've got. Don't forget: after we are done here, I'll go finish Marcus and Gilligan. I will make sure you have enough company wherever you are going." He keeps trying to fuel my rage. "If you are not going to fight back, just let me cut you down so you can be with Miles and Zack's sister."

Shanti, I think. The darkness realizes I've let my guard down in that moment and takes control again.

I block his last attack and punch him back. I keep coming for him without a moment to lose, each time getting closer and closer to striking him down. He isn't slowing down; I am getting faster.

I am able to give him a few cuts but nothing good enough to put a stop to him. He swings, and I duck. I kick him in the stomach, and he flies back. I run toward him. He looks at his sword and activates his

VANTABLACK

modifications. He has fire and acid. He gets up before I can strike him down.

We keep striking our swords against each other, harder and stronger each time. We stop moving around to fight. We stand our ground. One of us is going to be struck down right here. The darkness inside me has taken over completely and controls my body. I'm unable to do anything. I am a passenger watching from inside my head.

The speed of my body and my strength grow each time our swords collide. Julius is still keeping up as I slowly widen the gap between us in strength and speed.

He lets out a scream. He is going to use all his strength on his next swing. I do the same. The darkness in me isn't just trying to kill him; it is trying to defeat him without any doubt of who is better.

Our swords collide. Julius's sword breaks with the impact. Part of his sword flies through the air in the direction of the wall. I'm only able to give him a cut along his chest. His sword modifications turns off. I extend my sword toward him. He knows he has no chance against me without a weapon. He falls to his knees as he stares at the floor.

He looks up to the metal ceiling of the bunker, past the lights above us. He knows his time has come. This is it for him. I grab my sword with both hands, and I swing to cut his head off.

Right before my blade reaches his neck, it stops. There is nothing stopping it. I keep trying to move it to end this. I try as hard as I can, but I can't move the sword at all. I suddenly notice everyone else around us is flying away in the air.

I didn't hear it, but now I see it out of the corner of

ZETA

my eye: an explosion. The blast is pushing everything and everyone in the opposite direction. Julius's blade hit the wall of electronics and explosives, causing the explosion.

I am lifted off my feet and fly backward, along with Julius. I can see everyone in the air, being pushed with immense strength, and then, with the same strength, we are all pulled toward the wall. A hole has been created in the wall, and it pulls us all into it.

Everything goes dark. My face is on the ground. There is sand all around me. I get back on my feet, but it is hard to keep my balance. A ringing in my ears starts to give me a headache. The darkness that was using my body as its vessel has disappeared, along with the strength and speed that came with it. My body feels all the pain from the fight; it is screaming in anguish. I feel dizzy, and my vision is having a hard time focusing.

I see Julius on his knees not far from me. He is saying something as he holds sand in his hands. The ringing in my ears doesn't allow me to make out his words. I look around for my sword. I still want to end it. It isn't over until it's over.

VANTABLACK

I see my sword near me, with the tip buried in the ground. I concentrate all my strength on staying on my feet. I can't grip the sword firmly. I drag it along with me as I walk toward Julius.

ZETA

My vision and hearing get a little better, and now that I am closer to him, I can hear what he is saying.

"You promised! All of this for sand," Julius says with tears running down his cheeks.

I have no idea what he is talking about. He sounds disappointed, as if his whole world has just shattered in front of him, revealing that everything he has believed in is a lie.

"You talk too much," I say to him as I struggle to grab my sword with both hands. My hands shake as I try to raise my sword.

"Please," Julius begs. "End it. Please!"

I am surprised by his request. I thought he was going to beg for his life. I swing my sword. I know there isn't any strength behind it, but I still have to give it my all to extinguish this chapter of my life.

As my sword swings down toward Julius, I am pulled back by my shirt. I land on my back, and my sword falls out of my hands. I have no strength left at all. I look to my side to see who has taken this moment from me. It is Marcus. He keeps walking toward Julius.

I do not understand what is happening.

Marcus takes a deep breath. "This is what you fought so hard for. You won, Julius. You destroyed everything around you for a dream, and now here we are. Who are we to take this prize away from you? Go embrace it whenever you are ready, because it's all you'll have from now on until the end of time. You are not to come back to the bunker. This is what you wanted."

I have never heard Marcus talk to anybody this way, with no feeling or regard at all. Julius has been torn down to nothing. He isn't a threat anymore. Talking to

VANTABLACK

him is like talking to the grains of sand we stand on. He has become a ghost.

I am mad at Marcus for not letting me end it, but I can't do anything about it. I am barely hanging on. The colonel and his men, along with King, help all the injured to get back inside the bunker.

Julius and Kristov's followers who are still alive are arrested. The leaders of the packs agree they will decide what to do with them later on. We all head inside. As I am being carried away, I see Julius on his knees, surrounded by sand and blood. This is his life. I see regret and sadness in his eyes, but it doesn't matter.

I try to keep my eyes open as I am carried away, but I pass out after reentering the bunker. My body is screaming; the pain is immense. I try to hold on, but there is no use.

Is this how I will die? I think to myself as I see nothing but darkness.

Fifteen

I wake up on the first level of the bunker. I have been away for a while. Eleonore is taking care of me. She tells me Marcus and Gilligan have come by to take turns watching over me while I have been unconscious. I get out of bed, even though Eleonore tells me it isn't a good idea. She helps me walk outside the building.

I see that some of the areas have been reconstructed. Some buildings are being torn down to be remade, and others are being rebuilt from what is left. Everyone has been working hard to make this place livable again. People keep living their lives as best as they can, trying to hold on to what they have left and deal with what they've been through.

Eleonore tells me about what is going on. Marcus has the survivors of the Tiger and Snake packs working on rebuilding what they helped to destroy. With fewer people in the bunker, there is enough food to go around for everyone. People have traded guns and swords for hammers and pickaxes. There is no fighting. They are all working for a common goal. I don't know when the bunker was last this peaceful, especially since most of our history has not been recorded.

The Fox pack have chosen a new leader, and King and the colonel try to keep work on schedule as much

VANTABLACK

as they can. Marcus has been leading the Wolves as Gilligan takes care of the market, helping those in need.

People have stopped thinking only about themselves and think of one another for once. The Vultures are given a place to stay and food to get back on their feet as they help with the bunker.

I think of the past wars these metal walls have seen throughout the years. *Was it always like this? A war started, and in the end, peace reigned until someone started the next one?* It is no surprise most of our history has been lost. Books are the last thing anyone would think of saving in a war. I realize that no matter what I do, it will be as if I was never really here. I'll be forgotten like the people before me, both the heroes and the villains who've had their battles here.

Eventually, my body recovers enough for me to walk on my own and be able to help out. The darkness inside me is asleep once again. I am numb to everything around me, and I try not to think of it. I walk the streets, remembering Shanti by my side. I long to see her helping someone like the day I first laid eyes on her. Sadness consumes me as I think of her as a chapter of my life that has been torn away to make room for more stories.

The day comes when we are almost done with all the buildings on this level. I am working on repairs to a building near the one I used to live in before the war. During my break, I walk across the street. My old building is the next building to repair after the one we are doing at the moment. I make my way to my old life. The door is missing, and most of the things inside are broken or missing. I look around and see the shadow of an old life that is forever lost. I see Shanti walking

ZETA

around the room just like when she waited for me to come back home from a long day.

She would welcome me with a smile and a kiss and then pull me to the table to eat with her so we could talk about nothing at all as time flew by. We would lie in bed, looking at the ceiling and thinking about our lives and how grateful we were that we had found each other. My heart is heavy as I look around the room. I feel tears building up, but I am able to fight them and keep them from coming out.

I walk toward the furniture covering the hole in which I hid the backpack I found in the tower. The backpack is all that's left from my old life. I never thought it would be this important. I now cherish these items I found by accident, needing to hold on to what was once most precious. I had no idea at the time.

I walk out of the room with the backpack in my hands, making my way back to help rebuild the building we are working on.

During lunch break, Marcus comes by to visit. He has been checking up on me constantly since I left Eleonore's care. We talk about the irony in that I joined the Wolves to escape this kind of life and this kind of work, yet here I am. We laugh. He asks me how I am feeling, but the answer is the same as before: I don't feel anything at all. Emptiness and an indescribable feeling of numbness govern me. Whenever I do manage to feel something, I feel only sorrow and depression. He wants to help, but we both know it is something I have to manage on my own. I have always been honest with Marcus. It doesn't matter the question.

We sit talking past the usual time I take to eat my food. We laugh about old times when Miles was around

VANTABLACK

and talk of how everything is going with Gilligan. I haven't seen him much. He is always helping whomever he can, trying to stay busy, but also, he doesn't know how to be around me after everything that has happened. I don't take it personally. He is my friend, and I know it is hard for him to see me in my current state as I drift with no plan or goals. He is used to seeing a fiery kid run around trying to survive while dreaming of leaving this place.

"Can I ask you something?" I say as the conversation takes on a serious tone. "Why did you let Julius live and wander the outside world? Why not just end it?"

He takes a deep breath. He knows I have been wondering about this for a while. It was just a matter of time before I asked.

"It's easy to be dead." He pauses for a second, and his look seems distant. "Julius lived all his life by the words of an old man who thought he knew what the world was—his father. He trusted his word because he was his father, even when he did unspeakable things to him and his family. When Julius destroyed everything, he did it thinking he was going to find something he had been searching for his whole life. When I saw him kneeling in the sand, broken, I wanted to kill him and avenge Miles and everyone who was lost, but I knew it would have been too easy on him. The dead are just that: dead. Living is the hard part of existing. I wanted him to spend the rest of his days dying as he was that moment, so we left him there. I can't think of something more painful than being dead as you are still alive. Can you?"

Even though we are talking about Julius, I can sense Marcus is trying to tell me something. I am also dead while roaming the streets of the bunker. I help others

193

ZETA

and try to live a normal life, but how can I live a normal life if I am dead?

We stay silent for a second. He switches the subject to a more neutral one. He tells me they have found a door in the highest level that leads to a tower on each side of the entrance to the bunker. I grab the backpack I took from the room, which is filled with everything I found. I show it to him as I tell him the story of how I got to the top of the tower. I tell him to keep the backpack and all the items inside it. I feel I should let go of everything from my past to make room for the new things to come. Marcus smiles and tells me to keep the items. The other tower is filled with the same stuff. He says that everything in the room will be easy for him to replicate since there are manuals and blueprints of the items.

He gets up from his chair, as do I. We say our goodbyes, as he needs to get back to his tasks, and I have to get back to work. He hugs me before walking away.

Every day, I work as hard as I can on the repairs for the bunker. Some think it is because I feel guilty about everything that has happened, but that is a small part of the reason. In truth, I need to tire myself to be able to sleep at night. After talking to Marcus, I go back to work. I keep going after everyone else has gone, working until the lights go out in the ceiling of this level.

I walk back home with little light around me. Somehow, I'm not scared of the darkness or what creeps in the shadows. I know my biggest adversary is inside me, dormant, waiting for me to lose control again to try to take over. I crawl into bed after a hot shower. I lie there for a few minutes before passing out from all the work that day.

VANTABLACK

The mornings are still troublesome for me. Each day, I wake up to realize that Shanti is not here next to me and that everything wasn't a dream. I lie in bed for a few minutes, lost in my head, as usual. Something inside me wants to change the way things are.

I get ready for another day. I am about to head out, when, for some reason, I decide not to show up to repair the bunker today. I grab the backpack filled with things from the tower, and I walk all the way to the top level, where the entrance is.

I keep thinking about what's inside and how it could give me a chance to end it all against Julius. I don't know what to think of the darkness inside me. Is this thing lending me its power as long as it has control over me, or can I learn to wield it without having to give in to it? Will it destroy me in the end, or will it keep saving me, knowing that if I die, it will die with me? My mind keeps trying to reason it out, but I know I am not going to get an answer.

I finally reach the door to enter the tower. All those days of climbing the stairs make it easy for me to get here without realizing it, as I am caught up in my thoughts. I open the door. The doorknob has been removed. There are some stairs I have never seen before just in front of the door—a couple of steps that seem to be sealed off by a roof at the top of the stairs.

Marcus walks up behind me with silent steps. "It opens if you press this." He pushes a button next to the door. The roof at the top of the stairs slides open, making way.

Marcus doesn't ask me why I am here. He stands at the door as I walk up. I take a look around, remembering all the time I spent up here in this tower, the knowledge

ZETA

I gained, and the technological upgrades I stole from this room.

Once I met Shanti, the tower became less important to me as an escape from my reality. I always wanted to show Shanti the view from up here, but I never mentioned it to her. I feared she would think I was crazy for climbing up here.

I walk up to the glass to admire the view once again. The computer below me lights up. It is in the same place where I left it. The green mass on the map has kept changing size. Shanti's words resonate in my head. She wanted me to find a way to be happy. My hunger for adventure, which I lost after this ordeal, shows its face again. I take a picture of the map on the computer and print it. I fold up the paper, place it in my backpack, and then walk back down the stairs to meet Marcus.

We walk toward the hole in the wall that leads to the outside world, where Eleonore is standing with Gilligan. They usually meet here with Marcus and have breakfast together. As they wait on Marcus, they see us walking their way.

Eleonore smiles at me as Gilligan waves.

"I think I know what I want to do now," I say to Marcus as I keep looking forward.

He notices I am looking at the hole in the wall. "You don't know what's out there. Is there something I can say to change your mind? You are not going out there for Julius, are you?"

"I'm doing this for myself. For the first time, I'm doing something I want to do," I say to him with a smile. It feels strange. I don't usually smile. I used to smile only because of Shanti.

We finally reach Eleonore and Gilligan. Marcus

196

VANTABLACK

doesn't know what to say. Rapidly, they both pick up that something serious is happening, even though I'm smiling. They probably read it on Marcus's face.

"Is everything all right?" Gilligan asks.

"He wants to go out there," Marcus says before I can get a word in.

Eleonore just looks at me without saying a word. Gilligan is confused. He seems to think it is a joke, until he sees Marcus brush his hair back slowly with both hands as his stress rises.

"Why?" Eleonore asks. Based on the way she asks, I believe she knows it is going to happen but just wants to clarify my motive.

"I have always wanted to see what's out there. Since I can remember, these metal walls have felt like a cage to me, even as they kept us all alive. Now I have the chance to explore and venture into the unknown." I tell them enough, yet I keep part of the answer to myself.

I want to find a way to deal with myself and my darkness. I know there is no way to do it in here. I understand why they are scared, because no one knows what is waiting out there in the world that the people before us left behind. I know the darkness inside me won't let me die easily. If my biggest enemy is inside and I have to battle it every day, it doesn't matter where the battle takes place. I want to control the power that accompanies the darkness within me without losing control of myself. I want to see what this world has to offer before I can't do it anymore. I know that if I don't, I will always regret it. That's the difference between me and everyone else in here: I am willing to sacrifice my safe haven for a chance to live.

ZETA

Eleonore hugs me. Marcus and Gilligan seem surprised. Maybe they expected her to try a bit harder to convince me to stay. She asks for my backpack, and

VANTABLACK

she places the food she made for them to eat inside. I say my goodbyes as she places everything gently inside.

Marcus pulls out one of the swords he is carrying. He places it in my hands. It is the same sword he gave me the day the battle began.

"Keep this sword close. It will help you protect yourself from whatever is out there." He extends his arm to shake my hand. He is a strong man, and he doesn't seem affected by anything. When I hug him, he holds me tightly. I give him a smile, and he smiles back as a tear escapes and rolls halfway down his face.

As I turn to Gilligan, he is already stepping in to hug me. He nearly suffocates me. I never realized how strong he is. I almost feel my back snap from how firmly he holds me. He doesn't need to say any words. I know how much this means to him.

Eleonore gives me my backpack.

I pull out a hover board, put on the backpack, and climb onto the board. I am about to go, but something tells me to take another look back. As I do, I see the three of them standing there. "You guys have made my life worth it all this time. I hope you know that."

My words open the floodgates for the tears to flow.

"Don't forget to come back when your adventure is over," Eleonore says with a great smile.

I take off. The hover board speeds up. I pass the hole in the wall. I fly above the sand. I keep going. I feel the air around me for the first time in my life. As I keep going, I feel excited and at ease with myself. I don't know what awaits me, but it doesn't matter to me right now. Only one thought remains in my head: *I wish I could have shared this with you, Shanti, my love.*